A Summit in Shadow

~A Court of Mystery Novel~

Book Four

Sarah E. Burr

A brief history…

Centuries ago, the corrupt and powerful priests of the Ancient Faith lorded over the continent. Poverty and sickness ravaged the world, forcing a faction of rebels to rise up and overthrow these tyrants preaching in the name of silent gods. The leaders of this movement, known in the annals of history as the Rebirth, proclaimed the realm would no longer answer to nameless demons and gods, but to the virtues of bravery, humility, kindness, and intelligence. Under these Virtues, the world would once again flourish. Sealing their pact, these newly anointed leaders drank the dew of the fabled kingsleaf flower, ensuring their offspring would be marked as the divine protectors of this new era with their royal eyes.

Welcome to the Realm of Virtues.

The
Realm
of
Virtues
The
Brave Sea
Lysandeir
Cetachi
Pettraud
Kiwatalar
Mensina
Crepsia
Saphire
The
Sea of
Intelligence
The
Sea of
Humility
Laltor
Beautraud
Tandora
Hestes
Savant
The
Kind Sea
Isla
Delacqua

Chapter One

The crisp fall breeze swirled playfully around her skirts, a chill sweeping up her legs. Shuddering and wondering the cause for the sudden change in weather, Duchess Jacqueline Arienta Xavier pulled her woolen shawl tighter around her trembling shoulders. Just yesterday, she had gone for a ride down to the river, her horse panting in the fierce autumn heat. Yet, overnight, frost had formed on the ground, a reminder to her now that she could not escape the upcoming months of winter that lay ahead. Her amethyst eyes assessed the effect the frigid air had on her gardens, frowning as flowers wilted, their petals scattering the ground in a limp farewell to the summer months.

Oh, what a wonderful summer it had been, the Duchess thought, absently twirling the emerald and purple pendant hanging from her regal neck. She had spent most of the warm months celebrating, traveling throughout her duchy to announce, even to the most remote villages, that their mighty sovereign was to be wed. Looking down at the necklace bearing the colors of Saphire and Pettraud, Jax smiled at the memory of Perry's face when he asked for her hand in marriage. While initially their courtship began as an arrangement designed by their fathers, over the past year and a half it had blossomed into real love. As Duchess of Saphire, the most powerful nation in the Realm of Virtues, love and marriage rarely went hand in hand, but the Virtues had aligned and blessed her with a consort she cared for deeply. To her delight, but not true surprise, the rest of her duchy was thrilled that Lord Pettraud, the seventh son of Duke Pettraud, a neighbor to the north, was to become a Saphirian. It was hard not to like Perry, and everywhere they went, commoners and noblemen alike flocked to his side, eager to meet the new Prince Consort.

The thought of her fiancé calmed her nerves, for she had more pressing matters to attend to than her upcoming nuptials. Her brow wrinkled in disdain at the impending political summit that was to be held in little over a month's time. The castle had been a sea of chaos for the past week since receiving the summons, her royal advisors and courtiers arguing amongst themselves about Saphire's current position in the everchanging political landscape. Jax did nothing to interrupt their bickering, for their opinions meant very little to her regarding the matter at hand. Regardless of their arguments for or against, Jax's mind was already made up. Saphire would not accept the rebellious Cetachi as a true state unless a dukedom was to be formed.

For centuries, the most northern region in the Realm of Virtues had been a wilderness full of rogues and wild men, raiding and terrorizing the duchies on its border, spreading their terror out across the realm. There was no ducal family to rule, no laws of any kind binding the land. As a child, Jax knew her father had struggled but eventually obtained a peace treaty, offering food and supplies to the region to alleviate the raids that resulted from the desperation of the Cetachi people. Merchants from the north were allowed entry into the realm's marketplaces, selling their goods, helping stabilize the economy of the war-torn region. Because of these strides her father had helped institute, Cetachi had begun to pull itself out of its tribal ways and into a somewhat functioning society…a society that, according to reports, had elected a governor to oversee the region, but ultimately answered to the people who had elected him to the position.

The summit she was to attend was a gathering of dukedoms to meet with this new governor and review a proposition to adopt Cetachi into statehood. Or at least, that was the goal of Duke

Lysandeir, the ruler hosting the summit. As Cetachi's western neighbor, the snow-capped mountains of Lysandeir had been heavily assaulted by the rebels over the years. According to reports, the Duke was desperate to reach a peace agreement with this new figurehead that would be both binding and everlasting.

While Jax understood and sympathized with the man's struggles, she had studied diplomacy and politics since her early days at the Academy, and even before then, as a child at her father's knee. The masses simply could not be trusted to elect a true and just leader. Experience had shown her throughout her twenty-nine years that people could lie and manipulate their way to the top and easily fool the masses into securing power. What measures had been put into place to ensure Cetachi was not in the hands of some monstrous dictator, hellbent on revenge against the other duchies? Due to Cetachi's isolation, Jax had learned very little about this Darian Fangard, the newly elected Governor, and that lack of understanding scared her even more. Was this summit a well-laid trap, a plan to overthrow the ducal families and hold the realm hostage?

Many of her court advisors had suggested that she broaden her mind and be open to the proposed change. Cetachi's method of electing their leader was of no threat to the strongest duchy in the Realm of Virtues, so why should she protest the opportunity for peace? What these councilors didn't understand is that once word got out that the common folk held influence in Cetachi, others would thirst for that power, too, within their own borders. Jax shuddered to think of tensions rising between nobles and commoners, all wanting a stake in selecting who was to rule over them.

What her advisors failed to realize was that she had been born into her role, trained from the moment she could walk and talk to protect and serve her country. Had this Darian Fangard sacrificed his entire life for this new position? She highly doubted the man had spent years away from his parents and home, studying day in and out how to be an effective, gracious, and just sovereign, putting his duchy before everything else in life. No, the man had only recently come into power because of soothing words and brass actions, riling on the anger of the Cetachi people, divided and scattered across the region, looking for anyone to save them. No, she would not consider this man her equal on the political playing field. He was the end of a long, bad joke.

Jax was surprised to find High Courtier Jaquobie in her corner during her adamant refusals to accept Cetachi's requests for statehood. The shrewd and calculating man had served at her father's side for many years, and she knew it would be foolish to dispose of his services, regardless of how much she clashed with him. Her childhood memories were often dampened with visions of Jaquobie scolding her for breaching etiquette or forcing her to write lines for her childish indiscretions. Having the dark, amber-eyed man on her side made Jax question more than once if she truly was in the right, but her resolve stayed firm. She would go to Lysandeir and attend this summit, using her power and influence over her peers to make them see reason. From what she had gathered through various reports, her grandfather, Duke Mensina, would be in attendance, as well as her future father-in-law, Duke Pettraud. Both duchies were the strongest allies Saphire had, and Jax knew both men personally did not want to see an elected man ruling a nation. In the case of her grandfather, Jax often wondered if his motivations stemmed more from selfishness, than what was best for his people, but regardless, it made her happy to have him on her side. A few other duchies were sending High Courtiers in their stead, for many of the southern nations did not have direct conflict with Cetachi and thus were uninterested in this resolution.

The Saphire delegation would be small, but Jax had confidence in her companions. Besides Jaquobie, Lord Pettraud would be by her side. While of course she was bringing him because of his calming and thoughtful presence, she also planned to use her beloved Perry as leverage if Duke Pettraud became unmanageable. As much as she hated the prospect of using Perry as a bargaining tool, he understood this was part of his role as future Prince Consort. Her faithful Captain of the Ducal Guard, George Solomon, would be accompanying the group as well, along with a small squadron of men as protection. Her loyal lady's maid, Uma, and Perry's valet, Hendrie, would round out the delegation party.

Uneasy at the prospect of leaving Saphire's throne unmanned for a fortnight or so, Jax toyed with the idea of having Jaquobie stay and watch over the kingdom in her stead, but his arguments were too vital for her to leave him behind. Despite his unpleasant demeanor, he was a skilled orator and she would need his words backing her when she spoke at the summit. Even with Pettraud and Mensina's support, she would have her work cut out for her in attempting to align the rest of the duchies with her viewpoint.

A sorrowful chirping echoed overhead, causing Jax's attention to be diverted by the haunting melody of a white crown lark. The mournful cry was another reminder that the winter months were coming, sending unnecessary chills down her spine. The bird's song ignited a symphony of other peeps and chirps around her as she walked deeper into the gardens. The fluttering activity pleasantly surprised her, especially so early in the day. One creature's sound in the wind made her pause, unsure if she had heard it correctly. Attuned to the many indigenous species in her region, Jax knew the caw of a carrion hawk. "Why in the Virtues would one be near the palace?" she asked the walls of the stoic garden.

Hiking up her skirts so she could move more adeptly, Jax hastened toward the cackles that came from a small, private clearing off the southern edge of the garden. Pulling open the ivy-wreathed gate with a creak, Jax poked her head into the confined space. In the center of the alcove, a lone man sat with his back to her on a stone bench. Noticing his guardsmen uniform, Jax opened to her mouth to question why one of the Ducal Guard was taking a break in here. Her words caught in her throat as the black shadow of a hawk swooped past the man's body, screeching at Jax to back away.

Flustered by the man's obliviousness and the bird's demeanor, Jax reached for a branch, snapping it off a nearby pear tree. "Shoo! Shoo!" Jax batted the carrion hawk away with the leaf-bare branch, stepping closer to the hunched figure. He hadn't moved a muscle. "Sir, might I ask why you are in my grandfather's memorial sanctum?" Jax didn't bother to conceal her annoyance at the impertinence of the guard. This alcove was reserved for those in the ducal line for moments of reflection, not for the help to use during their shift change.

He still did not answer, nor did he turn around.

A cold hand of nerves seized Jax's insides, the branch trembling in her grasp. Her leaden footsteps halted as she moved around to face the guardsman. The sight of his bulging brown eyes shocked a shriek out of her, her hand whipping to her mouth to stifle the yell. She'd had enough run-ins with death to warrant a more dignified reaction to the sight. As she regained control of her breathing, Jax assessed the man's grotesque figure. The front of his uniform was caked with blood, which no doubt had attracted the carrion hawk. From his chest protruded the hilt of a golden dagger, the engraved amethyst and gold insignia announcing it was the guard's own weapon. Every member of the Ducal Guard was given one upon their induction. Examining the man's warped face, Jax found that she did not recognize this particular sentry, indicating that he was of lower rank and likely utilized to fortify the palace in some capacity. What was he doing here in the first place? Looking at the unruffled ground, she could tell he had not been dragged in here by his assailant. By the looks of him, he had been dead for quite a few hours, but considering the chill in the air, she could not be certain until her court physician, Master Vyanti, had performed an autopsy on the corpse.

Jax was about to run toward the small gate to call out to the guards stationed in the main area of the garden when a fluttering piece of paper pinned to the sleeve of the man's jacket caught her attention. Leaning closer, her curiosity nearly boiling over, the first thing Jax's violet eyes noticed was that the note was held in place by a dress pin…an odd accessory for a murderer to have on hand, indeed. Gently pulling the piece of parchment away from the blood-soaked body, Jax unfolded the note and looked at the contents. This time her shriek was harder to conceal. It felt like the earthen floor had opened up and swallowed her whole as she stared at the parchment, her entire body shaking at the implications.

She faintly heard a chorus of guards on the other side of the ivy wall calling out to her. "Your Grace? Your Grace, are you all right?" It only took a few heartbeats for Captain George Solomon to come crashing through the gate, his sword already drawn.

"Jax, what in the name of the Virtues happened?" One of her oldest and most trusted friends, George was unable to keep his familiarity with her in check as the rest of his men arrived at the small alcove. His dark brown eyes, indicating his common-born heritage, were a well of concern as he took in the scene, his face falling as his gaze settled on the dead man. "Marquis? What happened to him? He's supposed to be on guard in the dungeons." Standing at Jax's side, he took in her shock, her eyes still dazed with horror. "Are you all right, Jax? Did he attack you?"

His words finally clicking inside her head, Jax ardently shook her long, honey-colored curls. "No, no. I found him like this." She motioned to the glittering hilt sticking out of the man's chest. "You say he's supposed to be watching the dungeons?"

George nodded, bending down to examine the body with more thoroughness.

From behind them, one of the guards cleared his throat, his cheeks red as flame. "Actually, Captain, Marquis asked a few of us yesterday to switch shifts with him. I think Bernard ended up doing it."

George frowned at this news. "Isn't Bernard on dungeon patrol during the night?"

The guard nodded. "Yes, Marquis specifically asked to switch his day shift for one at night."

The knot in Jax's stomach tightened as she listened. She could see in George's eyes that he was trying to piece the puzzle together, but she held the last bit of valuable information in the clutches of her hand. "George," she whispered, forcing the Captain to lean in to hear her, "I found this pinned to his jacket." She held out the note for his eyes to scan.

As she expected, confusion laced his expression, not knowing what to make of the threat. "This means something to you, doesn't it, Your Grace?" He gazed at her with intensity, waiting for her to reply.

Looking down at the single letter gracing the page, Jax nodded, her eyes tearing up as she took in the sinisterly scrawled red 'A'. "Yes, I am familiar with this handwriting, George. It is a message from Aranelda."

Chapter Two

"Aranelda?" George choked back a breath. "Are you sure?"

Jax nodded with grave certainty. "We learned our letters side by side. She always had such a gaudy signature. How this came to be pinned to a dead man is the real question." Holding up the bloody parchment, she looked at the other guards assembled in the alcove. "I want the garden thoroughly searched and the palace locked down. No one enters or leaves without my express permission. Captain Solomon, please escort me down to the dungeons. I want to speak with the villainess herself," Jax commanded, her tone grim. She had not seen Arnie since the day she discovered her once-faithful lady-in-waiting had been part of a plot to kill her and take her throne…that her best friend was partly responsible for the deaths of her beloved parents.

"Why don't I go down and speak with her, Your Grace," George suggested as his soldiers marched out of the clearing, leaving them alone with Marquis's frozen body.

"No, I want to see her for myself." Jax's glare silenced any reply George had been forming. Sending a sentry to summon Master Vyanti to collect the fallen man, she stormed out of the garden, the tranquility of the cloudy morning shattered. With George at her side, she entered the dark halls of the palace, descending a path deep into the castle she was less familiar with. She did not make it part of her routine to visit the dungeons, and she was grateful when George took the lead without asking. While she found it somewhat surprising that he had acquiesced to her demands without a fight, she could tell he was shaken by what he had seen in the garden. Marquis, although a lower ranked soldier, was still a member of the Ducal Guard, and the loss of one of George's men would no doubt affect him more than he would willingly let on.

"Captain? Is something wrong?" A young man, whom Jax assumed to be Bernard, cast a questioning look at the pair as they arrived at the flickering flame-lit entrance to the dungeons.

"Did you see Marquis at shift change this morning?" Captain Solomon didn't bother with pleasantries or answering the bewildered guard's question.

"I didn't. He had taken off a bit before I arrived. He left a note saying he had to pick up some new armor before the quartermaster left for the night." Bernard shifted in discomfort under his commander's stare.

Growling, Captain Solomon pushed passed Bernard, throwing open the door to the long, hauntingly quiet passageway. Jax tried to give the young guard a soothing smile, but she was less than impressed that he had not reported his predecessor missing from his post. She knew George was beating himself up for the blunder, and decided not to mention the ineptness at the moment.

Following in the Captain's wake, Jax entered the dungeons. It had been years since she'd been in the belly of the castle. Shuddering in the chilly, damp air, she was reminded why she'd stayed away. The palace dungeons rarely held any prisoners; most criminals were dealt with in their own towns and villages. Even Sephretta, the capital city of Saphire, had its own prison. No, the palace dungeons were used for traitors and threats to the Crown. Jax knew that only two of the fifteen cells currently held inhabitants.

George grabbed a glowing torch, the light guiding them down the dark, cobblestoned hallway. On each side, Jax saw shadows dancing behind the bars of the spacious cells, dust and rot the only captives within sight. Up ahead, she could hear shuffling in one of the end cells. Her blood ran cold at the noise bouncing off the stone walls.

George held out a hand and took Jax's arm for a brief, protective moment. "Are you sure you want to see her?"

Nodding, Jax urged him forward. She heard him take a deep breath, and she realized that seeing Arnie this way would be difficult for him, as well. She wrapped her arm around his, squeezing it in reassurance.

Their pace slowed as they reached the final cell, the weight in Jax's chest making it almost unbearable for her to breathe. The noise they'd heard earlier echoing on the walls had stopped. The silence signaled that their appearance had been expected.

George lifted the shining torch up to the bars of Aranelda's cell, the light slicing through the blackness. Jax's eyes narrowed as she traced the perimeters of the cell, taking in the straw bedding on the floor with a small bucket in the corner. Even seeing it now, after all she knew Arnie had done, it still filled her with sorrow to know her former friend lived amongst this filth. Jax's gaze trailed along the stone floor, a woolen blanket strewn haphazardly to the side. Everything was as she had imagined it would be.

Except Arnie was nowhere to be seen.

George seized the bars and rattled them, the door to the cell swinging open in mock hospitality. "What in bloody hell!" he roared, storming into the chamber. He turned around, his rage heightened by the torch flames dancing across his face. "She's not here!"

Gripping the bit of parchment in her hand, Jax silently acknowledged that this discovery had not come as a shock. As soon as she saw the letter, her instincts told her that Arnie had escaped. And as to how, she could fathom a guess.

"Bernard!" George commanded. "Send the riders out; we have an escaped prisoner! Lady Aranelda has vanished, likely on foot, but check the stables to make sure she hasn't made off with a mount. Even with her head start, she could not have gotten far. She's weak from the diet we provide, and she would not have appropriate clothing for this type of weather. I want her apprehended and brought back...*alive!*"

"I once heard her say she had family out west who would take her in," hissed a voice from the shadows behind Jax.

She whirled around to face the other occupied cell.

The man staring back at her was gaunt and ragged, the years of his life spent in the dungeons aging him more than his nearly fifty years. Jax remembered the trial of this man, her first of its kind, when she was just nine years old. His dark, amber eyes had given her nightmares as a young girl. "Gabriel Reinbeck."

Recognition of the little girl-turned-Duchess flashed in the disgraced noble's eyes. "You remember me, then?"

Jax nodded, her expression hard as stone. "It's hard to forget the face of the man who hired a band of thugs to try and kidnap me so he could get my father to pay ransom for my safe return." She shuddered at the memory of the failed kidnapping attempt, which had been thwarted by the royal guards escorting Jax to a festival in Sephretta. On that day, a sixteen-year-old George Solomon had proven his worth as a member of the Ducal Guard and claimed her father's favor.

"I see that time has treated you better than it has me," Reinbeck said, his words dripping with stark malice. "But then again, maybe not." His amber eyes, the mark of his noble heritage, slid over to the empty cell where Arnie had once been caged. "She was a nasty one, but bloody brilliant. I didn't think her scheme would work, but she did it. She pulled it off." To Jax's stunned silence, he chuckled, admiration apparent in his expression.

"What did she do? How did she plan this?" Jax edged closer to the bars that separated her from her childhood tormentor.

"What's in it for me if I divulge this juicy bit of information?" Reinbeck asked with a weasel-like grin.

George stepped forward to stand beside Jax. "You get to keep both your hands." To emphasize his point, he pulled a gleaming sword from his belt.

Reinbeck eyed the taunting blade with unease, and Jax knew the man realized Captain Solomon hadn't spoken in jest. Spending the rest of his life in the dungeons with no hands would be significantly more unpleasant than his current miserable existence.

"Fine. Only because you asked so nicely." He licked his flaky lips before continuing. "The moment you threw her down here, she started scheming to get out. But as time passed, she grew more and more hopeless, moaning and crying all the time. The daytime guard,

Marquis, tried to calm her down, spending all his time sweet-talking, telling her everything would be all right. So much so that she fell in love with him and his naive assurances." He made a face. "It was sickening, watching them moon over one another. But it didn't amount to much. She got bigger portions of food, and he would sneak her fresh clothes every so often. But she never asked for anything in return. She said she knew she had done wrong and needed to be punished." Reinbeck stopped speaking to pick a phantom piece of grit out of his decaying teeth. "But about a month ago, she started prattling on, fantasizing about running away with Marquis and starting over in a duchy where they could be free without anyone knowing their pasts. I wanted to hang myself, having to listen to her go on and on about how much she loved the poor sod and how there must be a way they could be together." He rolled his eyes, seeming to relive the nauseating conversations in his mind. "But then things got interesting. She started hatching a plan, and she convinced the guard that he could unlock her cell, and they could spirit away in the night and start their new life. I couldn't believe how easily he agreed, especially knowing how noble and pure your Ducal Guards are supposed to be, Captain." Reinbeck spat at George, and Jax felt her friend tense at her side. "The lovestruck fool told her he'd stopped sending money home to his folks and was saving up for passage out of Saphire. She was very pleased by this, and she rewarded him very generously." He wiggled his eyebrows suggestively. "Last night they put their plan into motion. Marquis switched shifts with the night watchman, so that he could smuggle her out under the cover of darkness, and considering you don't have her in tow, it looks like they succeeded." He appraised his audience with a look of triumph Jax found disturbing.

"It doesn't appear there was ever really a 'they'. Marquis was found stabbed through the heart in the gardens this morning," she said, suppressing a shudder rising from the ugly ending of the twisted fairytale.

"Oh, she's even better than I thought." Reinbeck's eyes twinkled with mischief. "I may have lost count of my days, but faking a yearlong seduction does take stamina."

Jax grimaced. Arnie had been down here for more than a year, and during that time she'd been toying with some young boy's mind, just like she did during their days at the Academy. Jax recalled how Arnie had strung the Earl of Crepsta along with her cunning mind games, making him fall deeper and deeper in love with her with every passing moment. At the time, Jax believed it to be part of Arnie's charm and love of a challenge, but as she turned to stare at the empty cell behind her, she wondered if even back then there had been something more, something sinister, motivating her actions.

Reinbeck cleared his throat, interrupting Jax's reverie. "She did ask me to pass on a message to you, Your Grace."

Her violet eyes locked with his. "What did she tell you?"

Reinbeck paused theatrically, clearly savoring his lead role in this unfolding drama. "She said 'My games will not be ruined by the likes of you'."

Jax's cheeks burned. That phrase had hit her ears before, Arnie having said them herself. She'd spoken those same words long ago, in their suite at the Academy. Jax had just told Arnie off that she'd gone too far this time, coercing Earl Crepsta into stealing a famed relic from the school's archives, all to prove how much he wanted to escort her to the yuletide ball. Arnie had listened to Jax berate her schemes for hours. "The things you're making this poor boy do, it's not fair, Arnie. You should be reveling in his affections, not shunning them away and getting him to do these ridiculous stunts just to entertain yourself."

"You find them enjoyable at times, Jax. Don't make me out to be the bad guy just because I want us to have a bit of fun," Arnie had flippantly replied.

"I admit that at first I thought it was funny, seeing what he would do to get your attention, but now you've made a game of it. Enough is enough. If you don't stop this, I'll be forced to tell Earl Crepsta myself. I can't have this leading back to tensions between Saphire and Crepsta. There's too much at risk." Jax still remembered her reprimanding words.

Arnie's look could have frozen water midstream. "My games will not be ruined by the likes of you, Jax." A dark tension that had never been there before now hung between them. But then, with a bright smile, Arnie shrugged. "But you're right. I'll tell him tonight that I accept his offer to court me."

And that had been the end of it. Jax had never given those heated minutes another thought. They had the time of their lives at that yuletide ball. Jax had never seen Arnie so happy, so glowing as she'd been by the Earl's side that opulent night. Had that been when her plans began to form? Was she planning even then to take down the Xavier bloodline and claim Saphire as her own? The thought of a decade-long deception made Jax feel ill.

As fear and rage trembled with violence in her veins, she knew she had to remain calm for now with Reinbeck's eyes locked on her in a curious stare. Obviously, he did not know how Arnie's words would affect her, and she could tell he certainly did not expect this.

"We need to go," Jax said tersely, grabbing George by the arm and yanking him away from the man he had helped imprison.

"We're just going to leave him?" George stuttered, incredulous at Jax's dismissal.

"He's got nothing more to offer us. He clearly doesn't know where Arnie took off to. She has no family out west. Her bloodline descends from the eastern border of Saphire." Jax stopped briefly, eyes narrowing on George's bewildered expression. "I will overlook all the inept decisions made by men you have trained over the years if you are able to bring Arnie back to me." Jax left a shocked Captain of the Ducal Guard in the wake of her billowing skirts. As she ascended the dark staircase leading away from the dungeons, she yelled over her shoulder, "And I don't care if she's brought back alive."

Chapter Three

Jax's fingers tapped on the armrest of her golden throne, staring blankly across the imposing hall. Alone at last, she let the hard wall around her shatter the moment the guards closed the grand doors behind them.

My games will not be ruined by the likes of you.

Shuddering on her throne, Jax swore she could hear Arnie whispering the poisoned words from the shadows of the room.

The windstorm of emotions churning inside her boiled down to one thing: rage. Her anger at Arnie for pulling this desperate stunt ran so deep she could hardly breathe. Jax had half a mind to behead the fallen woman the moment she set foot back inside the walls of the palace. Not only was she outraged by slaying of an innocent man…no, her true anger came from the fact that Arnie had made the Ducal Guard and Saphire look incompetent and foolish. If word about this got out with the impending summit looming, her credibility and leadership would take a serious blow. She could not afford a moment of weakness with the future of the realm on the line.

A creaking door shattered her reverie, jarring her from her brooding thoughts.

"Jax? What is going on around here?"

The soothing, deep voice pulled her back from the abyss in her mind, and the Duchess's violet gaze focused on the stunning figure of her Prince Consort as he emerged from the shadows of the hall. Lord Pettraud, the seventh son of Duke Pettraud, marched with concern down the length of the throne room, his unruly dark hair sweeping above his lavender eyes. Just seeing him relaxed the tightness in Jax's shoulders, her stern expression melting away, for there was no other she would let into her fort of solitude but him.

Her throat constricted as she answered. "Perry, it's been a nightmare."

He reached her side just as she stood, scooping her up in his strong arms. Trying hard to keep her regal composure, Jax explained her walk in the gardens and the disastrous series of events that marred the morning.

Eyes wide, Perry knelt beside her throne as she sat back down, processing all she had shared. "It's still hard for me to believe that Arnie could be capable of such deception, even after her role in your parents' death," he said with a shake of his head.

Though the pain of it was still raw, Jax did not shy away from the subject. "Arnie was not a mere pawn in the scheme." Her eyes flashed. "I know we initially thought Earl Crepsta orchestrated it all, but Perry, I truly believe Arnie was the real mastermind. Reinbeck delivered a haunting message to me down in the dungeon, straight from Arnie's lips. It's led me to believe she thinks this has all been a game, and she is simply making her next move." Jax's voice trembled at the notion.

Perry placed a hand on her arm. "With last night's frost, she'll have left a trail leading away from the castle. I'm sure they'll be able to track her down on horseback, even with her generous head start." With his fingertips, he tilted her chin to meet his ardent gaze. "This will all be over soon, my love."

Jax nodded half-heartedly, begging the Virtues for Perry to be right. "The stablemaster reported that none of the horses are missing, so we know she left on foot, likely climbing the walls from within the garden. We used to do that when we were children." Her memories danced before her. "The ivy made it easy for us to haul ourselves over the barrier." Looking down at her lap, Jax felt tears well up behind her eyes. "I wonder if even back then, it was all a game to her."

Perry appeared to be searching for soothing words of comfort, when the main doors of the throne room burst open and Captain Solomon barged in. His cheeks were red from the cold, or perhaps from the embarrassment this whole debacle had caused. "Your Grace, apologies for the interruption, but we have word regarding the prisoner Lady Aranelda."

Jax rose from her throne, but did not descend the stairs. Scanning his face for any hint of whether the news was good or bad, her hands formed white-knuckled fists. "Please report, Captain."

George hurriedly beckoned a quad of soldiers shifting uneasily behind him to follow him to the base of the throne. "I'd rather the men speak about what they saw for themselves, Your Grace."

Jax looked expectantly at the worn-out guardsmen, knowing they must be exhausted from their pursuits. "Tell me what's happened," she snapped, unable to control her patience any longer. "Where is Lady Aranelda?"

The oldest of the guards stepped forward, assuming the mantle of messenger. "Your Grace, our quad investigated the western walls of the castle. We found footprints toward the southwest hedge of the garden and were able to follow them on horseback through the forest. It took us about an hour to catch sight of the prisoner, just as she was about to cross the banks of the Saltrine Lake. She covered an incredible amount of ground for being so poorly outfitted."

Jax stiffened with surprise. The Saltrine was miles away from Sephretta. Arnie had indeed gone a long way on foot. "Where is she? I want her brought before me now," Jax commanded, locking eyes with George. To her shock, the Captain of the Ducal Guard looked down at his feet, his shoulders hunched with a weighty emotion.

"You see, ma'am, we surprised her," the guard continued. "We had her cornered on a ledge overlooking the water. She...she scrambled backward, and apparently she slipped. She fell over the cliff and down the embankment into the lake. She hit her head along the way. There was blood...a lot of blood," he reported with a strangled gasp. "I believe the rock must have crushed her skull. We tried to get to her, but she fell into the deepest part of the lake. The depths claimed her. She...she did not resurface." He made eye contact with the Duchess, an aging worry on his face. "Lady Aranelda is dead, Your Grace. Her body lies at the bottom of the lake."

"You're sure?" Perry asked, his voice hoarse.

"We waited for her to come up for air, sir. She never did," the solider replied, his tone affirmative.

Jax held up her hand, effectively ending the conversation. "I want her brought back to me. I don't care if it takes hours to fish her out. I want to see her for myself."

The guardsmen exchanged wary glances, looking to their captain for confirmation.

Jax felt George's questioning eyes assess her. She turned her attention to meet his sharp gaze, her lips set in a thin line. "That's an order, Captain."

His expression told her he didn't have the heart to put up a fight today. Giving her a stiff bow, George beckoned his men to follow him out of the room.

"Jax, do you really think it's necessary to send them to fetch the body?" Perry asked, sounding rather put out by her morbid request.

Her violet eyes flashed to meet his. "In the matter of an escaped traitor, yes, having the body in front of me is *quite* necessary."

Perry stepped back, stunned by her severe tone. "Well, I'll leave you to your thoughts until they return, then," he said, hurrying out the door.

She regretted her reprimand the moment the imposing door slammed shut. Jax knew he was only trying to spare her the pain of what was to come. Sinking down in her chair, she felt the knots of dread multiply with each passing minute. Closing her eyes, she tried to push away visions of Arnie lying at the bottom of the Saltrine, but she was unable to escape her vivid imagination as she became lost in her thoughts.

‡

"Your Grace?" Captain Solomon's voice interrupted her self-inflicted confinement hours later, startling her as he reentered the throne room. "Have you been here all this time?" His tone softened as he took in her worn expression.

Jax dismissed his concern. "Did you find her?"

George took a deep breath before meeting her regal gaze. "Yes. We found her tangled up in some frozen reeds. Jax," he paused, lowering his voice, "are you sure you need to see this?"

Her nod was barely perceptible as she rose from her seat once more. "Bring her to me."

With a flick of his hand, George motioned unseen guards into the cavernous throne room. Three uniformed men appeared carrying a large bundle swaddled in wet burlap. Jax saw the outline of a human body pressed against the rough fabric, her stomach almost vaulting out her throat.

With deference, the three guards placed the drenched wrapping at the bottom of the stairs, each sending unsteady looks George's way.

The Captain met Jax's firm stare once more before signaling the guards to remove the cloth, unmasking the contents inside.

Jax had seen death many times, but nothing prepared her for the sight before her now. A tattered prison dress clung to warped body, water seeping from the pale, bloated skin. The Duchess's horrified eyes traveled over malnourished arms and matted chestnut hair, halting as she reached the face. Or what remained of it. The rock had completely smashed the skull, leaving bits of flesh here and there, and not much else.

As she examined the mutilated remains, a muted hush settled over the room. Jax couldn't seem to make out the clear shapes of people and objects around her; everything floated in front of her in a murky haze. Her eyes scanned the room, trying to find someone or something that she could bring into focus, but it all appeared to pool around her as she processed the mangled body.

"Duchess." Appearing from the shadows, she felt Perry's hand move toward her, but as she turned to him, she couldn't see his kind eyes clearly, either. Her whole world was encased in a dull gray shadow.

Arnie was dead.

Until the death of her parents, Jax had little experience dealing with personal loss. Her paternal grandfather, the Duke of Saphire, died when she was very young, a dim memory in the tapestry of her childhood. On the other hand, her parents' deaths had ripped the floor out from under her. Considering Arnie was the reason they no longer stood at her side, Jax thought relief and satisfaction would blossom from the news of Arnie's demise. After all, she had ordered the woman brought back to her dead or alive. But Jax had never seriously thought about a world without her childhood friend…let alone at the hands of the Saltrine, a place where they had spent much of their childhood, exploring every inch of the banks and splashing in the waters. She knew the cliffs the guardsmen had described. Death's Bluff, they called them as children, knowing the dangers of the steep rocks hanging over the deepest part of the lake. Picturing Arnie plummeting from those cliffs sent a shiver of hurt and betrayal surging through Jax's heart, threatening to tear it in two, proving that even after all this time, she still loved the person she'd thought Aranelda had been.

As if commanded by invisible strings, Jax felt her body lower into the throne, sinking deeply in the highbacked chair. "Thank you for retrieving her, gentlemen. Have her body prepared to be delivered to her family," she heard herself saying, her voice sounding like it was coming from somewhere very far away. "You are dismissed."

Wrapping Arnie's body with deft hands, the three guardsmen quickly exited the cavernous room, leaving Jax with George and Perry, both of whom looked at her with concern.

"Jax, I'm so sorry," George said, his face a mask of horror and sorrow.

"You are dismissed," Jax said pointedly to her captain, not bothering to acknowledge his apology. Her blatant command forced him to retreat, his head hanging low.

Perry again reached for her arm, only to have her shift away.

"You are dismissed," she snapped. His touch sent jolts of pain to her very core.

She saw the hurt and bewilderment in his eyes, and she knew he had every right to be confused by her feral reaction. She was the Duchess of Saphire, after all. She was supposed to be calm and collected in the face of adversity. But in that moment, all she wanted was to be left to grieve alone, to be weak in front of no one but herself.

‡

She wasn't sure how much time passed as she sat there, her back straight up against the cold, cruel throne. She was aware enough to notice daylight being overthrown by shadows, a gradual dark settling over the room as starlight began to twinkle through the high glass windows.

"Your Grace?" A timid plea called out from a side chamber reserved for servants. "Jax? You've been in here for hours. Everyone is worried about you." Uma's voice hardly contained her own anxiety for the Duchess's erratic behavior.

Gripping the armrest with force, her knuckles whitening with tension, Jax tried to swallow the lump inside her throat. She opened her mouth to shoo Uma away, but found her voice failing her. Her mouth was dry as the deserts of Zaltor. The food and water that had been placed at her side lay untouched.

"I have a bath waiting for you in your chambers, Your Grace." Pale and slender Uma arrived at her side, her commoner brown eyes glistening with tears. "I'm sorry for what the Virtues have dealt you today." Reaching out, she gripped Jax's arm with resolute tenderness and gently pulled the catatonic Duchess to her feet. "Come on, let's take you upstairs."

Jax thought vaguely about protesting her friend's attempts and ordering her out, but gave in to Uma's surprising strength and allowed herself to be escorted out of the dark throne room. The castle hallways were empty, the lateness of the hour meaning everyone was likely tucked away in bed. Only a few guards on patrol crossed their path, every man meeting her gaze with a curt, uncomfortable bow.

"Tell me, Uma," Jax said in a voice that seemed stripped of life, "how widespread is the news?"

"About Arnie?" Uma paused before asking, "Or about how you're reacting to it?"

Grinding her teeth together, Jax cursed inwardly. "Both, I suppose."

Uma's words came out tentative and guarded. "I believe Jaquobie is spinning the story in a new light, with the hopes that Arnie's escape from the palace will not surface. The official report is, that due to an impending threat, the former lady-in-waiting has been put down for the sake of the duchy."

Jax snorted. "Put down? She wasn't an animal, for Virtue's sake."

Uma unlocked the door to Jax's suite and led the Duchess inside. "It's a lot better than admitting members of the Ducal Guard let a traitor escape," she snapped.

Jax raised an eyebrow; normally, Uma was not so forthright with her opinions, nor so hot-tempered. "Is something troubling you, dear one?"

Uma sighed, wrapping her arms around her petite frame. "The guards kept me locked away in here when they were searching the castle. I had no idea what was going on, only that there was a threat on your life. They kept me in here for nearly two hours without any word of what was happening or whether you were even all right." Tears crept to the surface of her warm, dark eyes, and her words tumbled out in frantic alarm. "I was worried about you, Jax. And I guess I'm just drained from it all." Uma sat in a plush armchair situated by the roaring fireplace in the apartment's sitting room. "I know Arnie was a dear companion to you for many years, but I feel like I got to know her really well, too. It's tragic, what happened to her, but truth be told, I'm glad she's dead. If she had harmed you in any way, I would have strangled her myself." Her tear-brightened eyes watched the shadows, scrutinizing their every move. "How someone so blessed by the Virtues could descend into madness…well, it makes you think."

Jax took a moment to digest Uma's honest and open concerns before replying with hesitance. "Are you afraid that this all happened to Arnie because she was close to me? Are you afraid the same thing will happen to you, that I drive people mad?" Silent tears at the horrific realization pulsed down her cheeks as she whispered into the darkness.

Uma sprang up from her seat, rushing to her side. "Goodness, no, Jax! I wasn't trying to fault you at all." She squeezed the arm of her sovereign in a fond gesture. "It just makes me realize that putting your faith and trust in someone can be risky." She gave Jax a wry smile and added, "Not everything is about you, Duchess."

Jax managed a weak laugh at Uma's frank remark, grateful to the Virtues for her friend's heartening presence.

"Now, shall I put some hot stones in the water to warm it back up?" Uma stepped back, re-claiming her role as a lady's maid.

Nodding, Jax stood and wandered through the archway into her bedroom, shedding her clothes for the day. Looking at her perfectly pressed pillowcases, it was hard for her to believe that her walk in the gardens had only been this morning. It felt like days ago.

Gazing out a window at the tendrils of frost already crawling up the pane, Jax pictured the look of betrayal on young Marquis's face. She'd seen his despair in the garden, frozen in death, the realization that the woman he loved had just been using him. How agonizing it must have been. He must have welcomed a swift demise.

Minutes later, she lowered herself into the marble basin that sat in the center of her regal washroom. With closed eyes, she inhaled the relaxing scent of lavender burning from a small dish in the corner. She wanted to let the day's worries wash off her, but Arnie's parting words played over and over in her mind. *My games will not be ruined by the likes of you.* Macabre visions of the gory scene in the throne room loomed in her thoughts, and a grim expression settled across her face.

The game is at last over.

Chapter Four

Fastening her white fur cloak around her neck with a sapphire clasp, Jax gently pulled up her hood, so as not to disturb the tier of expertly woven ringlets perched on top of her head. "Well, I'm as ready as I'll ever be," she murmured with stifled confidence, assessing her gorgeous traveling gown in the mirror.

While she appeared every bit the radiant Duchess, it was hard to overlook the sorrow lingering in her eyes as thoughts of Arnie's grisly death still haunted her. Even though over a month had flown by in a blur of activities preparing for the summit, she still found herself in quiet moments like these reflecting on the gruesome ending to Arnie's life.

From behind, Uma emerged from the sleeping area in which they'd spent their fourth and final night of travel. She paused, seeing the Duchess's conflicted expression. "You'll be the envy of the realm, Your Grace."

Warmth crept back to her cheeks as Jax teased, "I already am."

Smirking while she folded the last of their traveling clothes back into their fine leather bags, Uma brushed non-existent dirt from her hands in victory. "There, everything is all set. I'll go collect Hendrie and have these brought down to the carriage so we can be on our way."

Grabbing one last pastry seductively sitting on a tray that had been brought up from the kitchens, Jax nibbled on the sugary morsel with thoughtfulness, surveying the cozy room they'd spent the night in. "I doubt these covert stops at roadside inns were what Perry had in mind for a visit to his homeland. I think he's disappointed that he hasn't been able to show me around where he grew up." Although, all they had done was sit in a carriage for their entire journey, so it wasn't as if this could really be considered an official visit.

Uma patted her arm. "I imagine some event will see us back in this area sooner or later."

They shared a wistful smile, making their way out of the Aldereen Inn's premier suite. Since leaving Saphire five days ago, the royal delegation had spent each night at a different inn or villa along their route to the capital of Lysandeir. Captain Solomon and a squadron of men had ridden ahead each day to secure a location and ensure the Duchess's privacy and safety. The Aldereen Inn was located on the border of Pettraud and Lysandeir and would be the final stop before arriving at the hosting palace later that afternoon.

"Sleep well, you two?" Perry's voice announced his appearance from down the hall, where he and Hendrie had shared a room.

Nodding, Uma slipped past Perry, leaving the two starry-eyed royals alone to enjoy each other's company. "I'll find Hendrie and meet you down at the carriage, Jax."

Perry watched Uma retreat with a grin on his face. "He'll smack me for telling you this, but Hendrie's absolutely smitten with her." He took Jax's hand in his own and gave it a reverent kiss. "He couldn't stop talking about how radiant she looked at dinner after we retired last night."

Jax gave him a conspiratorial look, her heart racing just by being so close to him. "I think she feels the same, but Uma's more cautious and guarded with her emotions. Wouldn't it be something if they, too, ended up together?" Hendrie, who was Perry's valet, was also one of his closest friends and confidantes, and therefore, Jax had grown close to the young, straw-haired man. "We're quite the little team, aren't we? Maybe we should start our own matchmaking service? Who do you think we could stick Jaquobie with?"

Perry's snorts of laughter were interrupted by a shadow down the hall.

"Thank you, Duchess, but I do not require your assistance in that department." A tall, rake-thin figure emerged from a nearby doorway, Jaquobie's shrewd face glaring at the two with undisguised disapproval. Although, when Jax thought about it, she wasn't sure if she'd ever seen the man look any other way.

Jaquobie approached them, his oily dark hair swinging in rhythm with his long, deep violet robes. The bronze medallion hanging from his neck, bashing against his bony chest, declared his position as High Courtier, the most revered and senior advisor in a royal court. Jaquobie had risen to his post before Jax's birth, having been a brilliant scholar and trusted friend of her father's when he attended the Academy, the famed university in the Realm of Virtues. How her kind and benevolent father had come to befriend such an odious man was still one of the mysteries that plagued her. Despite his less-than-warm personality, Jaquobie was the shrewdest political mind she knew, which was why she chose to keep him close to her court. She also believed he was not above betraying Saphire should she remove him from his position. Thus, their relationship had always been a balancing act.

"I've instructed Captain Solomon to send a few of his men ahead to announce our impending arrival. I want to ensure that Duke Lysandeir shows Saphire the respect it deserves with a well-attended welcome." Jaquobie, ever the man to deal a back-handed compliment, chose to refrain from saying that Jax was the one who deserved that respect. At twenty-nine years of age, she was the youngest ruler in the realm, yet her duchy was foremost in political influence, economic prosperity, and wealth. Many feared that with the deaths of Duke Saphire and his wife, the nation would crumble under such young leadership, but Jax had continued to develop her father's policies and the region had only grown stronger. Not that Jaquobie would ever admit it or give *her* credit for it.

"I'm sure Duke Lysandeir will be on his best behavior, Jaquobie. After all, he's sure to do everything in his power to try and sway my vote," Jax reminded him in a stern tone. If she changed her mind and sided with the Accord, others would be certain to follow her lead.

Not bothering to respond, Jaquobie gave a faint bow before following the path Uma had taken downstairs.

"Remind me again why you're so dead set against this whole Cetachi thing," Perry said as he took her arm and led her down the steps. "Hendrie and I have been debating the Accord, and it seems like a delightful experiment in free will."

She gave him a reprimanding look. "I have explained to you many times why we cannot allow Cetachi to elect its leaders. Ducal families are nurtured from birth to rule. How can we allow a man who hasn't even attended the Academy to be in charge of running a nation?" She sighed at the nugget of disagreement she still saw in his lavender eyes. "I know you believe differently, Perry, but I need you to tow the Saphire line. I can't have my betrothed seen as my opposition."

He grimaced at her retort. "I understand your point, Jax, I really do. But I also don't see the harm in letting people decide the fate of their own lives. Let them run the region into the ground with this new governor; they'll learn from their mistakes and rebuild to something even greater."

Jax rolled her eyes at the idealistic thought. "And what happens in the meantime while they are figuring it out, Perry? The whole realm falls apart. Commerce and trade are upended, people rebel, and we're left picking up the pieces. Why try to fix what's not broken? The dukedoms work, and they work well. Cetachi is the only nation that refused to be organized in such a way, and look at the chaos that's ensued in the region for centuries!"

Perry held up his hands in surrender, as if sensing that Jax's volatile temper was nearing its boiling point. "I know that, believe me. Pettraud borders Cetachi, and my people have experienced those pains for years." He looked down the hall with a haunted gaze. "I just wish it didn't have to be so black and white."

Jax softened her tone, meeting his hopeful eyes. "In matters like these, we can't afford to blur the lines, Perry. We must remain strong, for our people and for the realm."

He didn't answer, and the silence hung heavily between them.

Sighing, she left him to brood in grand foyer of the inn, seeking out Captain Solomon to arrange their departure. She found the regal guardsman chatting with the inn's proprietor.

Smiling demurely, she pulled George away, giving the innkeeper an apologetic look for disrupting their conversation.

"I was just giving my thanks for superb accommodations and adherence to our security measures," George explained, causing Jax to snort in a most unladylike manner.

"I'm sure the proprietor was more than willing to oblige considering how much gold we paid him," she said, rolling her eyes at the whole process. She knew it was for her own protection, but reserving every available room at each place they stopped for overnight lodging had put a dent in her treasury that she didn't deem necessary.

Normally, George would try to convince her that these were all essential measures, but he'd been walking on eggshells around her in the weeks following Arnie's death, and she suspected he did not want to force an argument. "Shall we prepare for departure? I've sent men ahead to announce our arrival at the palace."

"Jaquobie told me." Jax made a face as she recalled the unpleasantness of the encounter. "This summit is going to be nothing but glorified brown-nosing by the other duchies. How Lysandeir plans to change any minds is beyond me."

"He'll do what he can to target you, Jax. If the Duke can convince you to see things his way, everyone else will fall in line," George said, his worry evident about the measures the Duke might be willing to take.

While agreeing that the Duke could very well try and persuade her, Jax was more concerned about the resolve of the other leaders attending the summit. "I wouldn't be so sure about that, George," she admitted with a frown. "Of course, my grandfather and Perry's father will adhere to our agreement, but I can't say that I hold much confidence in the other duchies if Lysandeir is able to make them an offer they can't refuse. I believe Duke Crepsta will continue to side with us, after how things played out with his nephew..." Jax trailed off, shuddering at the memory, "but let's just say I'm not counting all my chickens before they hatch. Savant and Isla DeLacqua did not even send representation to the summit." She rolled her eyes, offended that her colleagues to the south chose not to treat this Accord as a serious threat to the stability of the realm. "I do wish Lady Carriena had been able to convince her father that their vote was worthwhile, but he already sent his abstention."

"With two duchies abstaining, the Cetachi Accord needs six votes for approval, then?" George asked.

Nodding, Jax explained the current political landscape. "Jaquobie's informants tell us that seven of the duchies are planning to vote against the measure. However, I think if Lysandeir strikes the right deal, Beautraud and Crepsta may falter, as they are our weakest allies at the moment. Hestes and Tandora have already agreed to the terms, so there is a chance we will have an uphill battle on our hands." She nervously massaged her arms under the shelter of her cloak. "I hope I'm up for it," she said, knowing this was going to be the first large political hurdle she attempted without her father's guidance.

George placed a comforting hand of her shoulder, his warm dark eyes crinkling with a smile. "You'll do fine, Jax. There's nothing you can't do if you set your mind to it."

She could see a ghost of regret in his eyes. "George, please stop blaming yourself for what happened to Arnie. I'm tired of all this useless tension between you and me. It's over and in the past. She deceived us all, used us all. It's time to let it go." She broke away from his pained gaze and stared beyond everything in the room. "She's gone."

George's shoulders slumped, and she knew that he, too, had been close to the woman they all considered a friend during their younger years. "I can't believe how it all played out. I...I feel like a failure," he stuttered as his words caught in his throat.

She returned the comforting gesture by giving his muscular arm a tight squeeze. "When this summit is over, we will have time to properly mourn all that we lost. But for now, we must focus on the future and security of Saphire."

"How do you do it?" George asked in stark wonder. "How do you box it all up and package it away?" He analyzed the calm mask she wore on her face.

Recognizing his sincere bewilderment, Jax knew he didn't mean to offend her, but his question nonetheless suggested he thought her void of emotion. "I don't have much of a choice in matters like these. I must be strong for the duchy."

Studying the faint sadness in her eyes for a moment, George answered with an affirmative nod. "I'll prepare the men for departure and have your carriage brought around, Your Grace."

Jax silently thanked her Captain of the Ducal Guard and wandered through the halls of the spacious inn, looking for her other companions. She ran into Uma and Hendrie just outside the dining hall, both looking flushed, their cheeks bright red from either the biting cold or the topic of their whispered discussion that trailed off upon seeing her approach.

Saluting her with an impish grin, Hendrie's brown eyes twinkled. "The bags have been brought down, Your Grace. We're just waiting for the carriage to come around."

Jax's keen eyes darted between her two friends, wondering what she had just interrupted. "Thank you, Hendrie. George is having it brought out now. Might you join Uma and I inside the coach today?"

Hendrie shook his head. "Many thanks for the offer, Your Grace, but even in this weather, I prefer to ride outside. The fresh air keeps the queasiness at bay." He motioned to his stomach, which became agitated any time he rode in small, confined spaces.

"You and George with your motion sickness. It's a wonder I take you anywhere," Jax said with a teasing laugh. Captain Solomon, too, found that any type of transportation other than walking or horseback left him feeling ill.

"Master Vyanti gave me some herbs to try this time around, but I'd rather not risk it to begin with. I want my stomach in tip-top shape for the feast tonight. Jaquobie told us that we've been invited to a meal separate from the formal dinner, but I've heard that the head of the palace kitchens is from Savant. Should be edible, I think." Hendrie gave Uma a sheepish glance before continuing. "I'll see to it that the trunks are loaded up." With a slight bow, the young man disappeared down the hall.

"I hope I didn't intrude?" Jax asked Uma with feigned coyness. She was bursting to know what might be going on between her maid and Perry's dashing valet.

Uma's pretty face blossomed to an impossibly dark shade of red. "We were just talking about how neither of us has been to Lysandeir before, that's all." Her warm eyes narrowed, silently beseeching Jax not to query her further.

Folding her arms as if expecting more details, Jax tapped her foot, raising one eyebrow. "Well, I don't know why you are eager to visit. It's a snowcapped wasteland, which is why I've kept away from it myself."

Uma looked surprised. "I've heard that the fortress is a marvel. The most secure in the realm."

This wasn't the first time Jax had heard this about the palace in Lysandeir's capital, Croivast, but she still bristled. "I'll remind you, Uma, that as a representative of Saphire, we must never concede that another duchy is better than our own in any way."

Uma's lower lip quivered for only a moment before nodding. "Of course, Your Grace."

Jax gave her a tight smile, but could tell that her curt reprimand stung. Even though she considered Uma a close friend, she had to remind herself that the young woman had been brought up in a small village without any formal training regarding the ways of the royal courts. Of course, Uma had learned quickly at Jax's side through the years she'd been in the royal family's service, but every now and then, she needed a reminder of how to act appropriately.

"I'll go check your suite one last time to make sure I didn't forget anything," Uma mumbled with contrition. She curtsied before backing away from the Duchess.

Sighing at her less-than-tactful misstep, Jax retreated to the foyer, where the rest of the Saphire delegation gathered. She bid good morning to the assembled soldiers who'd spent night and day protecting her throughout this journey.

"Duchess, if I may?" Jaquobie said, emerging from the shadows of the grand hall to pull her back toward the darkness. "When we arrive at court, might I suggest you interview Lady Lysette for the open position as your lady-in-waiting?" The High Courtier looked at Jax with piercing amber eyes, urging her to heed his suggestion.

"Why on earth would I make that offer to a stranger?" Jax hissed in hushed tones, hoping no one else overheard their conversation.

"You've delayed long enough in appointing someone. With Aranelda's death, we can finally move past this horrid business, and what better way than filling the position?" Jaquobie pressed. "It is not right for a Duchess to go unattended, especially for as long as you have. It makes you appear fragile, as though you can't move past the incident."

"And by incident, you mean my best friend and her lover betraying me by killing my parents and trying to steal my throne?" She couldn't believe Jaquobie was accusing her of being weak in the face of Arnie's crimes. It wasn't her fault that no one suitable enough had come forward to apply for the position.

Jaquobie looked past the venom in her eyes. "There is a royal wedding to plan now, meaning it's high time you had someone else attending to your affairs."

Jax felt her cheeks burn with indignation. "My lady-in-waiting is supposed to be my most trusted companion. You want me to appoint Lysandeir's daughter to the post, with all that we're up against at this summit? Are you mad?"

"Most trusted companion? How did that work out for you, Duchess?" Jaquobie said with a scowl, clearly not afraid of her temper. Pulling his robes tightly around his slender frame, he continued in a much more calculated tone. "Imagine how far offering the position would go, especially during these talks regarding the Cetachi Accord. Perhaps we can have Duke Lysandeir dismiss the whole matter by extending an invitation to his daughter to join the Saphire court and making a pledge of additional resources for border protection?"

Pushing her ego aside for the moment, Jax paused to consider the strategy the political mastermind proposed. "By additional resources, you mean my soldiers?"

Jaquobie nodded.

Jax's mind processed the plan. "I hate the thought of sending Saphire men into foreign mountains to fight off Cetachi rebels." She clicked her tongue, pondering the consequences. "But I would be tempted to loan the duchy a small company of guardsmen, granted our men train Lysandeir's warriors to be more effective so that we can eventually withdraw any physical support." She paced a short distance before returning to the shadows where Jaquobie lurked. "I'll consider it, after I have met Lysette and vetted her character. For now, we move forward as originally planned," she ordered, ignoring the scowl that briefly flashed across her High Courtier's face at her verdict. Even though his taunts of weakness left her ego bruised, she would not be bullied into making such a weighty decision. After all, her last choice for lady-in-waiting had nearly cost her her life.

She heard a chorus of horses nickering outside, signaling the arrival of her gold-gilded carriage. The guardsmen parted for her as she marched out of the foyer of the inn and into the raging cold weather. The winter months were now well upon them, the snowstorm announcing its arrival with a vengeance. The wind whipped at her fur-lined hood, cold flecks of snow and ice pelting her exposed skin. Overnight, the world around them had turned into a frozen tundra. She muttered a curse, for she knew it would only get colder as they crossed into Lysandeir.

Perry appeared beside her, offering her his arm. She used it for support as she stepped into the warmth of the carriage. Once inside, she turned to give him a grateful smile, but he had already retreated to his horse, his brooding figure buried under layers of wool and fur. Frowning at his sullen attitude, she turned to survey the spacious compartment where she would spend the remaining hours of their journey north. Fur skin blankets covered nearly every surface, and she quickly burrowed into them, taking a seat by the window. Uma climbed in after her and the carriage door shut with a snap. The rest of her delegation would weather the ride on horseback.

"Won't they all freeze out there? The storm is taking a turn for the worse, I fear," Uma fretted as she looked out her own window.

Jax glanced at her friend's reflection in the glass, seeing concern for the horses in her brown eyes. Reaching over, she gave Uma's arm a reassuring pat. "I sent a small envoy to Lysandeir a few weeks back, before the season changed, to purchase horses specifically for this trip. There is a merchant in the mountains who breeds animals accustomed to nasty weather like this. They'll be fine, dear one." It was so like Uma to be more worried about the comfort of the animals than the people they carried.

Uma looked away from the window to concentrate fully on Jax. "May I ask what Jaquobie was hounding you about just now? You looked miffed as you walked away."

Jax pursed her lips. "He thinks that offering Lady Lysette the post as my lady-in-waiting will somehow be enough to get Duke Lysandeir to call off this whole accord with Cetachi."

Uma's eyes widened. "Lady Lysette? But you don't even know her."

"I am quite aware." Jax leaned back into the cushioned headrest, her face set in a scowl. "I told Jaquobie I would consider it, once I meet her and see what she's all about...but I'd prefer not to go down that path. The position is too important to hand off to a stranger." At the sound of her friend clearing her throat, she turned to look at her, curious about what she had to say.

"Do you intend to fill the post with a Saphirian noblewoman, Jax? I'm happy to keep filling in, but I don't want to overstep my bounds if there is someone coming in to replace me." Uma became suddenly preoccupied with her hands.

With a long sigh, Jax looked out the window. "You're not going to be replaced, Uma. In fact, I'd be perfectly happy if things continued on the way they've been."

"With me fulfilling the duties of a lady-in-waiting?" Uma pressed. "Jax, why can't you just name me to the position and be done with it?"

The Duchess stiffened a bit at the edge of irritation in Uma's voice. "You know it's not that simple, dear one."

"Because I'm common-born?" Uma said with a quiet fire Jax had never heard before. "Hendrie has been asking me why that should be a hindrance if I'm the best person for the role?"

Jax sat up and looked at her sternly. "Well, Hendrie should know that a lady-in-waiting hails from a noble family. That's how it's always been, Uma."

"I told him that, Jax, and he pointed out how unfair that rule is. He's very passionate about the subject—why we common folk are stuck in the mud with our brown eyes. After all, we work hard to make the duchies thrive, and yet, we're still looked down upon by the nobles, and the ducal lines only deem us worthy to be servants." Uma's breath came out in a rush, as if she'd been afraid to stop talking until she voiced her thoughts.

"Where on earth is this coming from?" Jax demanded, never having heard her friend voice such concerns before.

"Hendrie and Perry discussed last night the new state Cetachi plans to build. Hendrie thinks it's a wonderful thing, where the people, common-born people, get to decide who their leader will be, where they have the chance to become leaders themselves. That in Cetachi, people will have the opportunity to throw off the societal chains and become more, not judged by where they come from, but by what they do." Tears filled Uma's chocolate-colored eyes as she spoke. "I know someone like you could never understand, Jax, but to live in a place where I could amount to more than a servant girl..."

Speechless, Jax gaped at Uma, who shuddered and turned her attention to the window, wiping away the tears that had sprung up from her fervor. Never, in all their years together, had Uma displayed such resentment at her station. She'd always been so timid and reserved. Jax found the young woman's sudden zeal nothing short of astonishing. "I didn't realize you and Hendrie felt that way," she said after careful consideration, "I hope you know you are more than a servant to me, Uma."

At that, Uma's face fell into her hands, her shoulders shaking with silent sobs. "Yes, ma'am, of course I know," she mumbled between gasps.

"I take it Hendrie has had quite a lot to say on the Cetachi Accord," Jax said with a calmness she did not feel. "Has this been your own sentiment for a long time?"

Uma shook her head. "I don't know. I've never really thought too much about it before. But after Hendrie told me what he and Perry had talked about and described this new way of life, I don't know, it...it triggered something inside me. Made me realize I want to be more than what I am."

Jax reached a delicate hand across the aisle to where her friend sat. "Who you are is a wonderful person. A person who is kind, intelligent, and brave. How does one improve upon qualities like those?" Her fingers entwined with those of her maid's trembling hands, hoping to soothe her.

Uma paused for a moment before pulling her hands away and clasping them on her lap. "I suppose it all has to do with wanting what you can't have." She gave her sovereign a self-conscious look. "I will go to my grave being mortified of this moment, I hope you know. I apologize for stepping out of line."

Jax watched an emotional barricade fortify between them as Uma regained her composure once more. "Please, do not beat yourself up for feeling strongly. I appreciate your honesty." She shared a smile with her friend, but could not dismiss the roiling in her stomach. With Hendrie fueling the fire, her beloved Uma reacted just as she feared others would when they heard about Cetachi's plans for statehood. If her calm, reserved lady's maid could have such a visceral reaction, it did not bode well for the duchies.

Yet, she could not get Uma's question out of her thoughts. Why could she not be Jax's official lady-in-waiting? What did being common-born really have anything to do with it? The question rolled around inside her mind as the carriage bounced along the icy roads snaking into Lysandeir, lulling her into a deep, unsettled sleep.

Chapter Five

"I've packed a light picnic, if you're hungry," Uma said with trepidation, offering a small platter of cheese and fruit to Jax as she shook herself from the clutches of a long nap.

"Delightful. Being inside a carriage this long always does make my stomach growl. This should tide me over until the welcome banquet tonight." Jax popped a grape into her mouth with enthusiasm. "Any idea where we are?" she asked as she surveyed the snow-covered landscape outside their bouncing caravan.

"Captain Solomon tapped on the window a little while ago to let us know we should be arriving at the capital in a few hours," Uma replied, taking a small bite of a pear slice. "In the meantime, might we do some wedding planning?"

Jax couldn't say no to the sparkle in Uma's eyes, especially after their tense interaction earlier in the day. She nodded her agreement, Uma barely containing a squeal of glee as she reached into her satchel to take out a roll of parchment and a quill.

"You came prepared," Jax observed with a wry smile.

"Your engagement was announced over five months ago and you still have not had an official ball to celebrate. When we return to Saphire that must be arranged, or the other duchies will take offense."

"I'm not sure why *me* not hosting a lavish party is a grave affront, considering it is *my* engagement and all." Jax playfully rolled her eyes.

"You're robbing the other leaders a chance to drink themselves silly. They would consider that an outright assault," Uma replied with a snort.

"All right, then. We'll plan something small. The noble houses of Saphire, a few friends, and the leaders of the realm. But let's not give anyone too much notice." Eyes dancing, Jax explained, "That way, they won't be able to come."

Uma frowned at her lack of enthusiasm. "You didn't seem to mind the attention of your engagement this summer. You toured nearly every village in Saphire without pause."

Jax pulled at the fur of her cloak, uncomfortable with Uma's line of questioning. "Well, being engaged was new and exciting then. Now, it's just turned into...a political circus."

Her friend's eyes narrowed, noticing the resentment in Jax's words. "What's really going on? Why have you been delaying plans for this wedding?" She looked around the coach, as if afraid someone might overhear them outside, and spoke in a near whisper. "Are you having second thoughts about Perry?"

Despite her frustration with his views on Cetachi, Jax laughed heartily at the thought. "Goodness, no. It has nothing to do with Perry." She became quiet, piecing her emotions together. "It's just, once we begin planning all these celebrations and ceremonies, I'm going to have to think about them without my parents being there." Her amethyst eyes misted over. "When you think about your wedding as a little girl, you picture your father walking you down the aisle, your mother fussing over your dress. It's hard for me to imagine the day without them, that's all."

Uma moved across the carriage, wrapping an arm around Jax as she reached her side. "I'm sorry, love. I know having them there in spirit is not the same as them being by your side. But I will make sure their memory is honored."

Jax wiped a single tear from her cheek, nervously tittering. "Look at me, getting all sentimental. Just think what a wreck I'll be when I have to walk down the aisle alone."

Uma tutted her displeasure. "Of course, you won't be alone, Jax.

Your father wouldn't want that. He'd understand you asking someone to escort you in his stead."

Jax felt a stab of guilt at the thought. "That seems crass."

Uma took her hand and held it tightly. "It is *your* wedding day. You could walk down the aisle with a trio of unicorns and no one would fault you for it."

Jax had to laugh at the image. "As magical as a unicorn escort would be," she paused as she looked out the window, the shadows of her guards trotting beside the carriage dancing across the snow, "why don't I ask George? He's always been like a brother to me, my protector, and my parents admired him greatly. What do you think?"

Uma's eyes welled with emotion. "Captain Solomon will be deeply moved, I believe."

"Then I'll find the right time to ask him. With any hope, it will finally make him realize I've forgiven him for what happened to Arnie under his command. A silver lining to this dreary visit." Jax released the caged glimmer of excitement she felt about her upcoming nuptials, allowing it to fill her chest.

"With any luck, we'll be back home in less than a fortnight. You have the votes you need," Uma said. "Just think of this summit as an opportunity to socialize with the other leaders." She seemed oblivious to the political turmoil brewing ahead of them.

Jax propped her hand against her cheek, releasing a mournful sigh. "I may have the votes I need now, but we are traveling into the lions' den, my dear. Cetachi has been a thorn in the side of the realm for centuries. The prospect of change might convince my peers to swing the other way, no matter what the cost."

"And you are certain this change Cetachi is advocating for isn't a good thing?"

Jax detected a slight barb in Uma's question, forcing her to think back to her friend's candid words at the start of their ride. "This isn't a battle between good and evil, dear one. It's a testament to what works. The ducal lines have ruled over the Realm of Virtues since the Rebirth, when the corrupted leaders of the Ancient Faith were relieved of their power over the people and the lands were free to live in enlightenment. We have had no wars, and our people are safe. The dukedoms work. Leaders are born and bred, dedicating their lives to the security of their respective duchies. I don't see how this new governor can hope to offer his people the same."

Uma contemplated the Duchess's words before nodding in agreement. "I guess I wasn't thinking about it in that light. You, too, have been born into a role that you cannot escape."

Jax waved the thought aside. "I am not asking for pity. I know I lead an exceedingly privileged life. But yes, I was born into this role; it is my sole purpose in life to see it done well. And I would consider myself a failure if I did not ensure that every person in the Realm of Virtues was under the protection of a good and gracious leader."

"Then what is your solution to Cetachi?" Uma asked, clearly intrigued.

"I want another dukedom to be formed."

A seemingly dazed Uma replied, "Another…How would that even happen?"

Jax leaned in and explained. "Well, the leaders would simply anoint a new Duke or Duchess to the throne. Most likely, we would select someone hailing from an established ducal family. I've been corresponding with my grandfather, and my Aunt Annette would be the ideal candidate."

Uma's eyes widened. "But she's in line for the Mensina throne, is she not?"

Jax bowed her head. "Yes, but she has three other sisters who could readily take her place under the tutelage of my grandfather. Annette has been groomed to lead for years; she could step into the position without hesitation. And then we would secure her rule with a marriage to, say, one of Perry's older brothers."

Uma's hand flew to her mouth. "Jax! How could you plot something like this? Selling your aunt off like a piece of cattle—I didn't think you had it in you."

Jax chuckled at her friend's shock. "It was actually Annette's idea. Apparently, after she saw how well my arranged marriage with Perry worked out, she was open to one herself. My grandfather has been trying to find her a match since the passing of her first husband, but only now has she agreed to the possibility."

Uma's cheeks flushed as she seemed to prepare her next question. "But your aunt is nearing the end of her childbearing age, is she not?

Wouldn't that make her rule unstable, if she's not able to produce an heir?"

At that, the Duchess of Saphire let a crafty grin slide across her serene face. "Then her rule would transfer to the rightful heir of the Mensina bloodline."

"Who would that be?"

"Me."

Uma's eyes almost popped out of her head. "*What?*"

"My mother was Duke Mensina's firstborn child, and therefore, the throne would revert to any of her offspring," Jax stated with proud finesse.

"Your grandfather would allow that? For you to swoop in and rule two duchies?"

Jax looked at her polished nails with disinterest. "I gave him a choice. It was either Cetachi or Mensina." She paused, taking Uma's bewildered expression into consideration. "By birthright, I am next in line to inherit the Mensina throne upon my grandfather's death. I simply offered to forfeit my claim to Mensina to one of my aunts in exchange for Cetachi."

"What a tangled web you've woven, Duchess." Uma brushed a strand of fallen hair out of her face.

"The bloodlines across the realm are all extremely blurred. Perry and I are hardly the first ducal lines to cross. Yes, there are a few leaders who have chosen spouses from noble houses to prevent things like this from happening, but you'd be surprised how many times duchies have changed hands over the decades due to birthright. My grandfather married a noblewoman initially to prevent his duchy being usurped from under his feet, but with my mother's marriage to my father, who was from an established ducal line, that was all put in jeopardy." Jax sat back, satisfied with her political prowess. "Luckily, Duke Mensina has such an understanding and sympathetic granddaughter."

"So, your proposition to the Cetachi Accord is to eventually place yourself as its leader?"

Jax frowned. "You sound like you think that's a bad thing, Uma."

Her timid friend looked out the window instead of facing her. "I don't mean to insult you, Duchess, but it just seems like a dangerous move in the midst of all the other leaders. Won't they protest you gaining so much power?"

"The initial proposition of seating Annette on the throne with a Pettraudian husband at her side does not look to directly benefit me in any way, other than my familial ties. I'm already bound to Pettraud through Perry, so on the surface, I look to gain nothing more than what I already have. And as I said before, half the ducal leaders are related in some form or another. Annette has already been inspected by a physician and has been told she has a few birthing years left, so no one will be immediately concerned about succession. My involvement wouldn't be likely to even be mentioned," Jax said matter-of-factly.

"And you think this scenario is better than letting the people of Cetachi pick their own leader?" Uma asked with an incredulous gasp. "Does Perry know that you're planning to have one of his brothers marry your aunt?"

Jax had the decency to look guilty. "I may have asked him if any of his older brothers would be interested in an arranged marriage into a revered ducal line, but I really didn't go into the circumstances behind it…nor did he ask."

"I doubt he'll be pleased you've been plotting this without his knowledge," Uma pointed out.

"I'll explain it all when our proposition is laid out before the summit," Jax reassured her. "If it even happens. Duke Lysandeir is desperate for the Cetachi Accord to succeed. Who knows what he'll promise the other duchies to get them to agree."

"Why is he so set on Cetachi becoming an elected state? Wouldn't he, too, want it to be a duchy?" Uma asked the same question that had first popped into Jax's head when she received word of the summit.

"The invitation he sent out to all the dukedoms explained that he'd met with the new governor and believed him to be a righteous and just man, and that the region was flourishing under his leadership." Jax rolled her eyes as she recalled the flowery language. "His main point was that this Darian Fangard brought about peace to a war-torn nation, so why wouldn't we want to legitimize it?" She paused, sifting through her buzzing thoughts. "I've never interacted with Duke Lysandeir, but I never guessed him to be the bleeding-heart-type."

"Well, it looks like we will find out his true nature sooner rather than later," Uma said, her eyes trailing outside the carriage as it rolled up a steep mountain. "Croivast looks inviting this time of year, doesn't it?"

Jax's attention turned to the imposing stone fortress rising above the snow-covered caps as their carriage finally approached the capital city. The palace was almost brutal in its design, making her shiver, the dark turrets rising against the mountains like clawing hands. "Ever so welcoming. Stay close to my side, Uma. We are about to enter the belly of the beast."

Chapter Six

The windows of their coach became encased by the white blizzard, the winds howling against the gilded frame as it rolled to a stop. Jax feared the strong gusts might very well lift the carriage right off the ground. Outside, she heard horses neighing and people shuffling about before they were jolted into movement once more.

"Duchess," Jax heard George's muffled voice call from the other side of the carriage door, "we're going to enter from the stables. The wind is too fierce to have you disembark outside on the palace steps."

Jax shot an irritated look Uma's way. "We're going to make our grand entrance through the stables? Are the Virtues playing some kind of joke?" She adjusted her fur cloak as the carriage once again rolled to a stop a few moments later.

Before she got a chance to look out the window, the ornate door swung open, revealing a lofty stable bay. Jax took Hendrie's snow-covered arm as she stepped out onto the straw-covered stone floor. Her eyes assessed the high-arching rafters, surprised at the spacious layout of the royal stables. She counted nearly thirty stalls lining the rock walls, leaving her with the sneaking suspicion that this barn had been built into the side of the mountain.

"Pleasant trip, I assume?" Jax said with a teasing whisper as Perry approached her.

As he lowered his ice-crusted hood, snow cascaded out of his hair, the dark ringlets frozen into place. "Quite the squall we ran into. I hope it clears up soon, or it will take some time to clear the roads for our journey back home."

It warmed her heart that to him, 'home' meant Saphire, although she was still a little miffed at him for the frank and forward discussion with Hendrie that had caused Uma so much angst. Her lips twitched, toying with the idea of reprimanding him, but decided against it. After all, she had warned him against voicing his opinion in public, not to his faithful friend and valet. If anything, Hendrie was the one with whom a conversation was warranted. "Those horses we bought for this journey certainly proved their weight in gold." She couldn't resist giving one of the majestic beasts attached to her carriage an affectionate pat, the animal's kind eyes reminding her of her own fierce stallion, Mortimer.

By now, her entire delegation had dismounted their saddles, everyone shaking their cloaks free of snow and ice. "I suppose we would have caused quite a mess in the entrance hall," Jax murmured to Perry, who knew she was not pleased by her less-than-grand welcome.

"High Courtier Jaquobie, is it not? We've been eagerly awaiting Duchess Saphire's arrival," a squat Lysandeir man said as he appeared in the looming doorway at the back of the stables, his attention directed to the head advisor.

Jax cringed at the use of the duchy's name as her own. Unlike many of her peers, she preferred 'Duchess Jacqueline' or the more formal 'Duchess Xavier' to the use of Saphire. It made her feel like a real person rather than a proverbial figurehead.

"Despite the detour we were instructed to take at the palace gates," Jaquobie said, his voice dripping with disapproval, "the Saphire delegation will be escorted to the entrance hall to be properly announced." It wasn't a request. "Please attend to Duchess Jacqueline and the rest of her party." Jaquobie gave Jax a quick look, indicating he knew she would want to be addressed as such.

"Of course, right this way, Duchess Saph—I mean, Jacqueline. This passage will lead us to the entrance hall." Their guide gave Jax a deep bow, his face beet red with embarrassment. "This storm caught us all by surprise. Nasty winds out there. Couldn't believe it when I woke up this morning and saw the snow nearly reaching my window. Many of the other delegations had to reroute to the stables, as well. That's why it was initially built to be so spacious; it makes for a covered entrance when the weather calls for it." He squirmed under her amused gaze. The middle-aged man obviously babbled when his nerves got the better of him.

Yet, she appreciated his reassurance that she wasn't the only one receiving this unusual welcome. "It is quite impressive, I must say. Built into the side of the mountain?"

He looked flabbergasted, either by her question or the fact she was engaging in conversation with him as he led her, Perry, Jaquobie, Uma, Hendrie, and George up a torch-lit stairwell. "The entire palace is built into the mountainside, Your Grace. Carved from the very stone of Mount Croie. Is this your first visit to our great nation?"

"Indeed. I have not had the pleasure of traveling so far north. My studies as a child took me to the southern ends of the realm."

"A child of the Academy, I assume? I have heard wonders about its sandy shores." Their escort's eyes glazed over with fondness.

"Yes, I had all my formative training there," Jax replied. "I'm sorry, sir, but I didn't get your name."

"Oh, silly me. My name is Courtier Roust. I will be High Courtier Jaquobie's liaison during your stay at the palace. If there are any concerns with your accommodations, please do not hesitate to reach out to me." He gave her a stiff bow, his round middle preventing him from bending very far.

"I'm sure everything will be lovely," she commented, secretly relieved that they had such a jovial courtier looking after them. More often than not, the position of courtier was filled by someone who thought rather highly of himself.

As if reading her thoughts, Jaquobie cleared his throat. "I do hope our delegation will have individual rooms whilst we are here."

Roust nodded adamantly, a bead of sweat forming between his amber eyes. "Of course, sir. Duchess Jacqueline and her guests will be in the west wing tower of the palace." Turning back to Jax, he smiled under his bushy mustache. "Just wait until you see the sunset behind the mountains, Your Grace. The hills sing."

Her eyes lit up. "That sounds like an absolute treat. I look forward to the storm dispersing so that I may see it."

By now, they had arrived at a large set of double doors, in front of which two uniformed guards in Lysandeir colors stood at attention. "Now, I know we have your betrothed Lord Pettraud with you, Your Grace, but is there anyone besides High Courtier Jaquobie that we need to formally announce?"

Jax turned to look at Uma and Hendrie, her mouth set in a thin line. Normally, a valet and lady's maid were not introduced in such a setting, even if they were their charge's most trusted companion. The thought flashed through her mind that if Uma was her lady-in-waiting, she *would* be announced. "That will be all, Roust." She risked a look back to see if there was hurt in either of her friends' eyes, but each wore a formal mask.

"Duchess, if I may, I will take a few men up to the west wing to inspect your chambers before your arrival," Captain Solomon said as he gently touched her arm. Leaning in close to her ear, he whispered, "In this den of vipers, I don't want to take any chances."

Looking at the innocence written all over Roust's face, Jax had a hard time picturing that this man could be masking something sinister, but she nodded and let her captain ease into the shadows of the stairwell.

"Once the Duchess is announced, she will retire to her rooms until the welcome feast," Jaquobie instructed Roust, who nodded vigorously, as if his well-being depended on agreeing with the advisor.

"But of course, sir. I will make sure to inform Duke Mensina that his request to meet with the Duchess will need to happen at a later time."

Jax's ears perked at the mention of her grandfather. "Duke Mensina requested a meeting with me?"

"Yes, Your Grace. He asked to see you in private after you'd arrived and were settled in," Roust reported.

"Tell him he may visit my apartment at his earliest convenience," Jax said, purposely avoiding Jaquobie's glare. He knew nothing about her grandfather's plans to seat Annette as Cetachi's ruler, and for now she wanted to keep it that way.

Roust bowed his head once again. "Now, pardon me as I

announce your group, Your Grace." With that, the man ducked out through an unobtrusive side door that would likely bring him to a steward's post in the entrance hall.

"Presenting," his voice boomed moments later, reaching them even through the heavy door, "the Illustrious Duchess Jacqueline Arienta Xavier of Saphire."

Jax and Perry shared a comical glance with one another. Each time she heard her name pronounced with such flourish, she couldn't stop the tingles it sent shooting down her spine.

Before her delegation, the large double doors parted, bright sunlight spilling into the royal chamber. Jax blinked a few times to gain her bearings, not appreciating the ambush of light in her face as she walked into the grand hall. As her eyes adjusted, she surveyed with a mask of feigned boredom the room encompassing her. Much like the stables, the stone walls and high ceilings arched overhead, the gray rock looking cold and uninviting, even in the daylight. She imagined this room would look downright spooky in the evening, bathed in torchlight. There were few furnishings within the cavernous space, and even fewer pieces of art. The only piece that stood out to her was a large tapestry draped from a ceiling beam, depicting snowcapped mountains. She recognized it from her texts at the Academy. It was meant to be a replica of a map drawn by the first northern explorers who discovered Mount Croie and its surrounding hills and was one of Lysandeir's most prized possessions regarding its heritage.

She now allowed her amethyst eyes to focus on the figures standing at attention in the room. She recognized the familiar faces of her grandfather and Duke Pettraud, whose resemblance to Perry was striking. Duke Crepsta's stooped frame stood near them as well. Each Duke was clad in his nation's colors, cloaks of fur falling off their shoulders, keeping them warm against the chill in the room. While she did not smile at the three men, she tipped her head in recognition before swiveling her gaze to the remaining figures she was not as familiar with.

Duchess Tandora, a striking, formidable woman, stood proudly, although her wrinkled hand clutched a golden cane. Her silver hair was twisted and pinned up, showcasing the waterfall of turquoise and citrine jewels cascading from her slender neck. Jax had seen the Duchess briefly at the Feast of Champions over a year ago, and in the past year the woman had aged with grace. Beside her stood a young matron with amber eyes, likely the Duchess's lady-in-waiting. Jax did not know her name, for she had not seen her at the Duchess's side before.

Jax reluctantly met the gaze of Duke Lysandeir, his fiery red hair making it impossible for him not to stick out in the grim-faced crowd. He stood at the top of the staircase that led back into the sprawling throne room of the fortress, elevating him amongst his peers. Jax resisted a frown at the petty power move, giving the Duke a tight smile instead. "Duke Lysandeir, thank you for welcoming me into your home." She glided up the steps until she stood level with the burly man, his sneer shrinking as she took her place next to him. "I look forward to these peace talks and the prosperity they will bring the realm."

Duke Lysandeir shifted on his feet, straightening out the fox fur wrapped around his broad shoulders. "Duchess Jacqueline, it is an honor to host such historic talks." His tenor voice was firm and strong, but the look of daggers in his eyes told her he did not appreciate how closely she stood to him.

Jax turned and waited for Perry and Jaquobie to make their entrances. She caught sight of Duke Pettraud as his eyes focused on his son for the first time since Perry's dispatch to Saphire. She knew father and son had a strained relationship, a chasm that only widened after the death of Perry's mother, but she was troubled by the lack of warmth in Pettraud's eyes as he studied his youngest son. She caught a quick glimpse of her grandfather, the imposing Duke Mensina, who, of all things, winked at her. If she and her grandfather could mend their once-strained relationship, perhaps the same could happen for Perry and his father.

"Duchess Jacqueline, I believe you know all the leaders here with us for the summit. Might I introduce you to our friends from Cetachi?" Duke Lysandeir held a swooping arm out to the stone floor below.

Jax's stomach seized with sudden anxiety, realizing George was nowhere to be seen, nor were any of her other guards. What was to stop this gang of wild men from launching an assault on the Realm of Virtues right here and now? Harnessing her worries, her eyes trailed to the shadow of one of the round pillars, from which a figure emerged into the light.

The man at the bottom of the stairs bowed, his sandy auburn hair sweeping forward to obscure his muddy brown eyes. "Greetings, Your Grace. I am Darian Fangard of Cetachi. It is an honor to be in your esteemed presence."

As Jax appraised the man before her, the confidence and refinement he exuded surprised her. He wore all black, save the gold threaded accents etched along the seams of his tunic. His pale complexion suggested he rarely saw the sun, but his skin had an ethereal glow about it, and his eyes shone with promise. He didn't look the part of a shrewd and manipulative politician, but more like a philanthropic humanitarian. "Sir Fangard, I am pleased to put a face to the name," Jax said. "We have heard much about you in Saphire." Her lips twitched with veiled sarcasm.

Fangard's polite response reflected no protest, but he managed to mock her just the same. "Please, Your Grace, call me Darian. I am but the son of a baker. The only title I hope to be known by is 'Governor'."

Jax bristled at the sparring words, but did not take the bait. She was not ready to discuss the future of Cetachi just yet.

Darian seemed to sense her hesitance, for he motioned his hand out to another shadow sulking behind him. "Let me introduce my friend, Maegus Welles. Should our peace talks be a success, he will serve as Warden of Cetachi's capital city."

Maegus proved to be a face that Jax expected to see from Cetachi. He had a long mane of wiry brown hair, his dark whiskers framing a snide smirk. He posed a looming figure behind Darian, burly arms folded under his earthy green tunic. Where Darian had a refined and polished appearance, Maegus was brooding and wild. The blazing intensity of his gaze alarmed Jax, as much as she hated to admit it.

"And what role does the title 'Warden' play in your vision for Cetachi, Darian?" She heard herself asking the question before she realized what she was saying. Jaquobie shot her an incredulous look. She wasn't supposed to be even entertaining thoughts about Darian's proposal for Cetachi.

The as-yet unappointed governor gave Jax a calculated stare. It wasn't one of malice, but one of curiosity that she'd bothered to ask him about his plans for his nation. "Well, right now, Maegus assists with the day-to-day tasks of making sure people within the borders of his tribe are protected and cared for. My vision is that each region of Cetachi would be overseen by a Warden, elected by the people living in those tribes. The Wardens would form a council, voicing the concerns of people across the land."

Jax studied the earnest look on the man's face. "And where does that leave its governor?"

Darian continued, his cheeks flushing with enthusiasm for his ideas. "Well, the council would report to me, so that I could ensure fairness across the regions and make sure any orders are executed properly."

"It seems like a waste of time and resources, having a council do the work of one person," Duchess Tandora declared from her post, tapping her cane on the floor for emphasis. "I decide what is best for my duchy, and no one else."

Darian stepped forward, but was careful not to ascend the staircase out of reverence. "Duchess Tandora, do you not employ advisors to help you determine what is best? My vision simply calls for those types of positions to be elected by the people."

"Because commoners are so smart and know what's best for them, do they?" Duchess Tandora snapped back, not giving Darian the respect he'd shown her.

Her reaction intrigued Jax, for she was under the impression that Tandora supported the Cetachi Accord. Yet, it didn't appear that its Duchess believed in the democratic ideals Darian held in such high esteem.

Duke Lysandeir jumped into the conversation. "Now, now, let us save this talk for tomorrow. I'm sure you all would like to rest before the welcome feast tonight." His silencing look at Darian put an immediate stop to the escalating argument.

Jax couldn't help but feel for the poor, idealistic governor who withered under Duchess Tandora's stare. "An excellent suggestion, Duke. Until then, I bid you all good afternoon," she announced to the room before retreating off to the side where Roust waited for her, along with the rest of her companions.

"Your apartments are this way, Your Grace," he said as he led her down the long hall with Perry, Uma, and Hendrie following in her wake. Jaquobie had disappeared from her side without her noticing. She wondered where he'd gone off to.

Roust led the way through the maze of passages and staircases with ease. "Your guardsmen took the liberty of delivering your trunks already."

"Brilliant," Jax said, longing to throw off her traveling clothes and immerse herself in a warm bath. Although, knowing her grandfather wanted an audience with her, she doubted she'd have long to linger in the soothing waters.

The sheer size of the Croivast fortress was proven by how long it took them to make their way to the west wing tower. Jax realized she hadn't paid close enough attention to Roust's skillful navigation, and she wondered if this was a trick imposed upon by their host to make them feel uneasy roaming the halls.

"I realize the palace must seem like a labyrinth to you now, Duchess, so I will come to gather you all before dinner and escort you to the dining hall," Roust said with a charming tip of an imaginary hat as they all arrived at two large blackwood doors. He pushed the brass handle, throwing the doors open to reveal a stunning interior.

Jax had visited many fine suites throughout her travels across the realm, and those of Lysandeir proved to be no exception. While it was minimalistic in decor, the impressive stone fireplace pulled everyone's focus to the enticing flames taking up nearly half of a wall. They entered a sitting room, adorned with a plush sofa and collection of armchairs, with doors leading into what Jax assumed to be a bedroom and bathing room.

"Lady Uma's room is just through this door here," Roust said, pointing over to an archway in the corner, "and Lord Pettraud's suite is down the hall. His valet will be in the room adjoining his, and your guardsmen will be in the remaining quarters on this floor," he further explained, although Jaquobie was not there to witness that Lysandeir had indeed complied with their requests for individual accommodations. "Shall I send for Duke Mensina?"

Pausing only a moment, Jax decided it would be better to speak with her grandfather now so she could spend the remainder of the afternoon resting after her journey. "Yes, please, Roust. That would be wonderful."

He nodded in affirmation. "The Duke is staying in the eastern wing of the palace, so I imagine you will have a few moments to catch your breath before he arrives." With that, the little man disappeared.

Perry let out a low whistle as he settled into one of the chairs by the fire. "That was an interesting reception if I've ever witnessed one."

"It certainly was. I must say, Darian Fangard was nothing like I expected him to be." Jax sat down across from Perry, rejoicing in the warmth of the fire as she shed her cloak.

"Dare I say there's a hint of admiration in your voice?" Perry teased, although his searching eyes watched for her true reaction.

Jax furrowed her brow. "I'll admit, I was impressed by his thoughtfulness. He obviously cares deeply about his cause. But his idealism is childish. A council where the officials are elected? Why, it's a breeding ground for corruption," she said with a sharpness that made Perry's body visibly twitch.

"But then the people would be free to overthrow that corruption and create a new council," Hendrie said, stepping forward from Uma's side.

Jax turned to face him, disliking his tone of voice. "Then the Cetachi people are forever left with a government continually cycling out its players, never getting any real work done. Or worse, perhaps these elected officials pass laws and ordinances that protect their station and their corruption only grows from there."

Hendrie opened his mouth to protest, but Jax held up a hand. "Please, enough. I know that you and Perry do not see eye to eye with me. Forgive me for saying this, but *I* am the one who leads a successful duchy, whereas you two do not. You have no idea the amount of work I put in to eradicate corruption across my lands. I simply do not trust Darian's method to work for Cetachi in the long term, and that is Saphire's official stance." Jax hated silencing her friends, but they were in someone else's home, where eyes and ears would be reporting their every move. She could not have whispers floating around that might hurt her plans.

Despite her forceful warning, Hendrie made moves to open his mouth and protest, but Perry cut him off. "Understood, Duchess. You are right. Neither Hendrie nor I know the stressors you deal with to keep Saphire safe and secure. I think we'll depart for our rooms while you speak with your grandfather."

She knew Perry hadn't meant to make her feel bad, but she saw a sting of anger lingering in Hendrie's brown eyes as he followed his charge out of the room. "Oh Virtues. Maybe I should have come to this thing alone." Jax sighed, resting her face in her hands.

Uma's hand gently touched her hunched shoulder. "They might not agree with you, Jax, but neither would they want you to bear this burden by yourself."

Jax looked up at her friend's innocent face. "Do you understand my point of view, Uma? The way Hendrie looked at me…I feel like some deranged dictator."

Uma bit her lip. "I do understand that you want what's best for the people. But I also think this Darian character wants what's best for his people, too. It's a difficult situation to reconcile, with both parties believing themselves to be in the right."

Jax raised an eyebrow. "I see Darian's charms enchanted you, as well. Do not breathe a word of this to the others, Uma, but I think the man has potential in the political arena. Despite being the son of a baker, he certainly knows how to command a room." She looked thoughtfully at the roaring fire. "I look forward to getting to know him better as these talks continue. There's something very intriguing about him." Jax leaned back into the chair, closing her eyes as she replayed the encounter over and over in her mind.

She could hear Uma moving around the apartment, unpacking and hanging Jax's gowns so as not to wrinkle them. She relished the moments of peace before they were interrupted by a knock on the door.

Uma rushed to the small entryway, momentarily disappearing from Jax's sight. When she returned, her face had developed a nervous tic. "Your grandfather has arrived, Duchess."

Jax stood up, smoothing her skirts. *And so it begins,* she thought.

Chapter Seven

"Jacqueline, my dear, I almost giggled with delight when you went toe-to-toe with ol' Lucien on the stairs." Duke Mensina chuckled as he enveloped his granddaughter in a bear hug, referring to Duke Lysandeir by his given name. "I thought Delphinia's eyes were going to pop out of those wrinkly sockets."

Jax pictured Duchess Tandora's expression and laughed at her grandfather's exaggerated imagery. "I hope that show was just for my benefit and that Lucien hasn't been making you all feel this way."

Duke Mensina stroked his trimmed gray goatee, his dark violet eyes scowling. "He wasn't even at the palace when I arrived last night. Didn't return until late this morning. Said he was on a hunting trip."

Jax rolled her eyes at the obvious lie. "Please, a hunting trip that kept him away from his duties as summit host? I hope you had your courtiers look into it."

The Duke gave her a look that practically shouted, *Of course.*

She motioned for him to take a seat before he divulged any more information, smiling with affection as he groaned into the cushions with old age.

"From what my spies, eh, *courtiers* have gathered," her grandfather said in hushed words, "Lucien rode out to meet and escort Maegus Welles to the palace." His kind violet eyes sparkled with deviousness as he delivered this news.

"What? The Warden didn't travel here with Fangard?" Jax looked taken aback.

"No, in fact, Darian arrived yesterday only an hour after I did."

"Why in the Virtues would Lucien step away from his duties at court to meet with a lowly member of an unrecognized government?" Jax's keen mind went to work trying to unravel the Duke's perplexing actions. "What ties does Lucien have to Maegus?"

"I asked Darian that very question." Her grandfather shifted in his seat, leaning forward. "He seemed to be just as surprised as I to find out the Warden would be joining us here at the summit. He had instructed Maegus to remain in Cetachi during these peace talks to look after things in his absence. The poor chap was furious to be caught off guard, finding out his second was being accompanied here by the Duke himself." His bushy eyebrows wiggled as he relayed the gossip.

Jax folded her hands on her lap, in awe of this new development. "What is Lysandeir playing at, then? Does he want to somehow seat Maegus as the leader of this supposedly free Cetachi?"

"The most unbelievable part of the whole ordeal was Lysandeir's excuse to Darian. He said that Maegus served in a position similar to a High Courtier, and since many of the duchies were traveling with or sending a High Courtier to the summit, Cetachi's should be there too," Duke Mensina recounted.

Jax's mouth popped open in disbelief. "How did Darian react?"

Her grandfather let out a hoot of dark laughter. "I'll give the boy credit for the poise he displayed. He must know not to bite the hand that's feeding him. He thanked the Duke for looking out for Cetachi's interests and left it at that."

"Very interesting," Jax murmured, scanning her grandfather's face for further details. "I'm going to keep a careful eye on that partnership. What else have I missed?"

At that, her grandfather cringed. "I spoke with the High Courtier from Zaltor this afternoon. He took a meeting with Lucien after he arrived from collecting Maegus." Duke Mensina paled for a moment. "Zaltor is changing its vote in support of the Accord."

"What!" Jax nearly leaped out of her chair. "How could this

happen?" Zaltor had always fallen in line with Saphire and Mensina. "What were they promised?" she demanded, remembering too late that her grandfather was merely the messenger of bad news and not its cause.

"You're not going to like this one bit, Jax," he warned, "but apparently Cetachi is willing to make the Ancient Faith the official religion of the region in exchange for Zaltor's support."

Jax felt as if the rug had been pulled out from under her. "Impossible. Why would Zaltor agree to such terms?"

Her grandfather shrugged. "There are many outposts of the Faith still functioning in Zaltor today. It may not be the official religion of the duchy, but its Duchess treads very lightly with the Order to maintain peace amongst both sects. From the sounds of it, the High Courtier is planning to offer leadership positions in Cetachi to some of Zaltor's prominent priests in exchange for consolidating the number of active temples in Zaltor."

Jax threw her hands in the air. "So, to the other duchies, it looks like Zaltor is finally closing the temples they promised to during the Rebirth, but in reality, they're just shipping the Ancient Faith to a new location." She began pacing around the room, her frustration nearly pushing her to heated tears. She had not expected Duke Lysandeir to stoop this low, nor for Zaltor to accept such a petty bargain. So much for her defense that dukedoms were less corrupt than democratic nations. "How did you find out about this?" she asked. She couldn't imagine the Zaltorian High Courtier would have shared this under-the-table treaty so willingly.

"Actually, our dear friend Darian told me about it during afternoon tea. He was very upset and let it slip. Mark of an amateur," her grandfather scoffed. "He believes the people of Cetachi should be free to believe in what they choose. He doesn't want an official religion slapped across the nation. He himself is a devout believer in the Virtues."

"But it doesn't sound like he's doing anything to stop it," Jax mumbled grimly.

"It was Maegus who persuaded him that all nations in the realm have an official belief system attached to them, so what was the harm in allowing the Order of the Ancient Faith to preach from Cetachi.

The ends justify the means, if you will." The Duke crossed his arms, not looking pleased. "Darian may be idealistic, but he knows he needs more allies. I'm sure it didn't take much to persuade him to come around to the idea.

Jax returned to her chair, feeling angry enough to rip apart the cushions beneath her. "Grand-Père, if Lysandeir manages to swing one more duchy to sign this Accord, our plans completely go up in smoke." She tried not to sound too overwhelmed, but she felt close to hysteria. Never had she thought Zaltor would switch sides.

"Ah, now, that is the reason why I came to speak with you in the first place. I have an amendment to our proposition." Duke Mensina's expression turned shrewd and calculating, his diabolical grin widening. "I may have only just met him last night, but I have spent considerable time conversing with Darian Fangard and hearing about this ideal Cetachi he has plans for. The man has charisma, that is certain, and he is passionate about allowing his people's voices to be heard." He stood up and leaned against the hearth of the fireplace. "Fangard simply wants the opportunity to let Cetachi flourish on its own. All these tricks that Lysandeir is pulling to make it so have left him uneasy. The stunt with Maegus, the Zaltor deal, he doesn't believe it to be right. It undermines what he believes in."

Jax resisted the urge to roll her eyes. "His naiveté is truly astounding. It's amazing he's lasted this long in the political arena."

"I concur, but—and I think you'll agree with me—I think he's worthy to be somewhat in the spotlight," Duke Mensina said.

"What do you mean?" Jax's eyes narrowed, sensing she was not going to entirely like the topic they were encroaching upon.

The Duke met her intrigued gaze head-on. "What if we made Darian Cetachi's leader?"

"Have you lost your mind, Grand-Père?" Jax laughed at the ridiculous notion of giving up on all they had planned. "Cetachi would descend into even more chaos, letting the people choose their own officials."

The formidable man wagged his finger back and forth. "Not as a leader chosen by the people, darling, but a Duke chosen by the realm's royal families."

Speechless, Jax couldn't find words as she stared at her

grandfather's apparent madness.

Sensing her astonishment, he continued. "We offer him the ability to rule his people as he sees fit, but within the confines of the institution we have thrived under for so long. My Annette would make sure of that." His chest visibly swelled with pride at his solution.

"You want to offer Darian Annette's hand in marriage *and* Cetachi?" Jax finally was able to pull herself out of her shocked stupor.

Mensina nodded, as if he wasn't planning to upend the very foundations of the realm. "I don't think Darian is the problem here. Lucien and Maegus are the ones fueling the rebellious fires." He paused to let Jax absorb his accusation. "My courtiers have been haunting the hallways since we arrived, and have all but confirmed Lucien wants Cetachi for himself so he can move out of this freezing hellhole and rule from somewhere a little warmer."

Jax's eyebrows nearly disappeared under her bejeweled crown. "So, you think the peace talks are all a front?"

"*Of course.*" Duke Mensina scolded his granddaughter for her thoughtlessness. "We all know how bitter Lucien has been since he took the throne. He spent his youth in Savant. You think a hotheaded man like him liked being dragged back to his ancestral home to rule in mounds of snow? He hates this land and would do just about anything to get away from it without losing his title."

"So, a vote for Cetachi is actually a vote for Lysandeir," Jax stated grimly, her skin paling. "Your courtiers are sure this is the plan?"

The Duke nodded. "And I don't know about you, but I'd rather see Mensina blood on the throne of Cetachi. Of course, that still includes you as well, my dear," he said with a tender but gruff look.

"What will Annette think of all this? Have you had time to reach out to her?" Jax felt a little dizzy from the upheaval in their plans.

"She's here at the palace. I brought her along. I figured our peers would be better off visualizing our solution for Cetachi if she was beside us," the Duke explained. "She met Darian at breakfast this morning. Sure, she's a little older than he is, but they got along well enough, and she's ready to do what it takes to ensure Cetachi doesn't fall into Lysandeir's outstretched hands."

The firelight danced throughout the room, painting the stone red. Jax shivered at the imagery of blood on the walls. "And what do you think our righteous governor would think of the bargain?"

At that, the Duke looked less pleased with himself. "The poor sod is determined to see his people have a voice. We could try to reason with him that Lysandeir is not an ally, but rather a snake waiting patiently in its den."

Jax considered the approach. "I'm sure if you painted the same picture as you've done for me of Lysandeir's true intentions, he'd at least have to step back and think about it." She thought back to the enthusiastic young man she'd met in the grand hall. He couldn't be more than five or six years her senior, and yet the entire balance of the realm rested on his shoulders. "Let's see how the summit begins tomorrow. If Lysandeir does not have the votes for the Accord, then we don't need to deviate from our current path. But if it looks like things are going to change for the worse, then we can approach Darian with our suspicions and make an offer." She studied her grandfather's face, which looked much older and worn out since she'd seen him last at their family's yuletide celebration. "Are we in agreement?"

"Of course, my dear." Duke Mensina cocked an eyebrow. "I assume Lord Pettraud doesn't know we've been having these little chats?"

Jax shook her head. "Nor does Jaquobie. The fewer people who know about this, the better. We don't need the other courtiers to catch wind of our plans."

Her grandfather eyed Uma's form moving about in Jax's bedchamber. "I trust your maid will be discreet with what she's overheard?"

Jax gave him a severe look. "Yes, Grand-Père, I assure you that Uma will not breathe a word of this to anyone."

"Then I'll let you rest from your journey. I look forward to sharing in this evening's shenanigans with you, my dear." Duke Mensina planted a quick kiss on Jax's cheek before he departed to his own chambers.

Jax had to smile at his small display of affection. If someone had told her two years ago that she'd be having these types of interactions with her imposing grandfather, she would have told them they were crazy.

Apparently, Uma was thinking the same thing. "My, how you two have changed around one another," she said as she entered the room, her eyes bright with intrigue. "I can hardly begin to process what I've heard. How awful for Darian that Lysandeir is simply using him for his own means."

"It is a bit heartbreaking, but Darian is a fool if he thinks Lysandeir's patronage comes without any strings attached," Jax replied. "It makes me so mad that Lucien is risking the security of the realm for his own gain. It makes my argument about allowing the people to choose their own leader completely moot. Corruption is everywhere, even in those bred for benevolent leadership." An immeasurable sadness welled up inside her. "Is this how you felt when I was describing my plans to rule Cetachi?"

Uma's hand flew to her mouth. "Oh Virtues, Jax, no! I know you were coming from a place of good intentions. You are a strong and fair-minded woman who rules her duchy admirably. Lysandeir is nothing like you."

Jax managed a grateful smile. "Let's just hope future-Uncle Darian sees it that way, too."

Chapter Eight

At long last, Jax sank into her warm bath, the smell of lavender oil tingling her nose. After her whirlwind discussion with her grandfather, she was in need of some alone time to sort out her thoughts. She had come here hellbent on ensuring Cetachi didn't fall victim to an age-old idealistic theory that never worked in practice, only to find out that Cetachi's failure at democracy was just what Lysandeir was planning on. She would find the time to speak to her grandfather's courtiers herself, to confirm what they'd heard about Lysandeir wanting to seize Cetachi. While she wanted to fully trust Duke Mensina, she couldn't ignore that he was still the leader of another duchy, playing the games of power for his own nation's advantage.

Jax thought about seating Darian, the son of a baker, as Duke of Cetachi. If a common-born man could rise to become Duke, perhaps this would pave the way for Uma to become her lady-in-waiting. It could quite possibly start a whole new movement across the realms, where offspring of royal families could marry whomever they pleased. While the thought of a commoner sitting on the throne may have shocked her ancestors, it filled Jax with an odd sense of peace. It might not be the voice of the people Hendrie proclaimed to want, but it was a step in the right direction to compromise.

Her thoughts were interrupted by a thud resounding from the

floor above her. She tilted her head, her neck resting on the porcelain tub as she studied the stone ceiling. Listening for further sounds of shuffling, she gave up after a moment or two. Perhaps there was another delegation on the upper floors of the tower. She hoped that her neighbors, whoever they were, would not prevent her from getting a good night's rest when the time came.

Jax made little effort to chat while Uma readied her for the welcome feast. She was too preoccupied planning how to survive the evening to be sociable.

If Uma was offended, she didn't show it. She painted rouge across Jax's cheeks and lips with nimble fingers, and at last set her honeyed curls into place. "I think we chose tonight's ensemble well," she said with satisfaction as she looked at the fully dressed Duchess.

Jax twirled girlishly around her room in a brilliant royal purple ball gown, dripping with glittering gold jewelry and wearing a most lavish crown atop her head. Although she would never admit it to anyone, she loved the pomp and circumstance of elegant dinners that required her to dress up.

"You'll have them all eating out of the palm of your hand in no time," Uma surmised with a wry smile.

"Beautiful work, as always." Jax cupped her friend's cheek with fondness before opening the door leading out into the hallway. "Enjoy your evening," she called back with a wink, knowing that Uma was looking forward to the dinner she was to attend with Hendrie.

As she came to the edge of the landing outside their spacious floor, Jax was pleased to find Courtier Roust ready and waiting for her arrival.

"Your Grace! My stars, I have never seen a beauty like yours," Roust squeaked in awe, quickly blushing at his outburst. The formal robes he wore denoted his position in the Lysandeir court.

She thanked him for the compliment, a genuine smile situated on her lips. "I hope we have not kept you waiting too long out here in the cold." She noticed that the temperature dropped drastically from what it had been in her room.

Roust chuckled. "Despite all the chambers with raging fires, it is always cold here, Your Grace. I believe my skin has formed a protective layer to keep me warm," he said, rubbing his round stomach in exaggeration.

Jax took the opportunity to dig for more information while she waited for the rest of her party to join them. Laughing lightly at the man's joke, she took his arm in hers. "I can imagine it's not always fun and games being trapped amongst the snowdrifts. I think I would go mad."

The jovial luster diminished in the rotund courtier's eyes. "Ah, yes, sometimes it does dull the mood, but Lysandeir people make the best of it. Most of the region's population relocates to the southern border during the winter months, when the weather is at its most fierce. Even Duke Lysandeir enjoys his trips to the balmier duchies when he can."

"Does the Duke spend a lot of time away from home?" Jax pressed, trying to sound causal in her line of questioning.

"He does travel more than his father did while he was Duke. I don't think our sovereign has a strong emotional attachment to this place," Roust surmised, unwittingly giving Jax the opening she needed. "I'm not sure what it is, but sometimes it feels like he's a caged, restless animal when he's here for too long of a time."

"Has he spent a lot of time in Cetachi, assisting Master Fangard with his plans for peace?" she asked with feigned innocence.

Roust shifted under her gaze, looking uncomfortable for the first time. "I know he's traveled to Cetachi on numerous occasions, but I am not privy to his reasons. I must be honest with you, Duchess; I only recently became a Courtier."

Interesting, Jax thought. She imagined she should see it as a slight that Lysandeir had assigned her such an unseasoned escort, but she was intrigued by the man's voluntary admission. "May I ask what you did before coming to the palace?"

Roust blushed. "Oh, I've been here for many, many years. Probably since before you were born. My father sent me to Croivast to study in the palace archives. I come from a noble Lysandeirian family with little money left to its name. My father couldn't afford to give me an Academy education, so he sent me here. The Duke's father was in power then. He set me to work in the archives with some of the historians. I'm somewhat of the resident expert in the

Rebirth, if you will."

Jax did not have to forge her impressed expression. "There are very few scholars left in the world who focus on that period of time. Even my professors at the Academy knew very little about the details of the downfall of the Ancient Faith."

Roust nodded solemnly. "Yes, unfortunately, because they think the past is over and done with. But as the scholars here always taught me, history is bound to repeat itself."

Jax found that proclamation odd. As she watched sweat bead across his furrowed brow, she dared a guess. "Do you mean to say you think the Cetachi Accord is reminiscent of the Virtuous Ones deposing the Ancient Faith?"

Roust's eyes crinkled, and he took a breath for what seemed like the first time in minutes. "Oh, you are a clever girl. I've heard tales about you, Duchess. You like to unravel puzzles, am I right?" He didn't give her a chance to respond. "I know as a Courtier of Lysandeir, I am supposed to support my duchy, but I'm worried about how these peace talks will turn out, Your Grace. When I heard you were going to appear at the summit in person, I asked the Duke to be your escort. Since that role belongs to a Courtier, I became one."

Jax's eyes widened. "You left your career as a scholar just so you could walk me around the palace?"

Jax knew Roust's eyes darted about the room to ensure they were alone. For once, she was grateful that Perry was running behind schedule. As to what was keeping George, she didn't know. Perhaps he still feared being alone with her and preferred to wait until Perry made his appearance.

The fear in Roust's trembling voice brought her focus back to him. "I think there is a devious plot afoot, Your Grace, and I want to help you solve it."

Her eyes widened. "Please, Sir Roust, you cannot say something so shocking and leave me without the details." Jax tried to be polite as she could, seeing that he shook with genuine distress.

"We don't have time speak now; they will suspect something amiss if we do not appear at the banquet soon, but if you can meet me in the library later tonight, I will explain what I know."

"Who is 'they,' Roust? Is the Duke planning something?" Jax

gripped the man's arm, silently begging him to speak.

"I don't know who it was I overheard, Your Grace. I was in the north tower doing some research before I came to fetch you just now. I heard voices in one of the side chambers. Something about causing chaos until certain demands have been made." Roust looked truly terrified as he recalled the memory.

Jax was about to question him further when the doors to Perry's and George's rooms opened and the men joined them in the hall.

Ever her protector, George seemed to immediately sense something was wrong as he reached her side. "Is everything all right, Duchess?" He eyed the courtier with suspicion, his jaw set in a hard line.

"Roust was just telling me that he believes he's stumbled onto some sort of vicious plot." Jax quickly brought her companions up to speed, despite the courtier's protests for secrecy. "Captain Solomon and Lord Pettraud have assisted me in such tricky situations before, Sir Roust. You can trust them as you do me."

"Whatever you say, Duchess, but we must get down to the banquet hall before Duke Lysandeir sends someone out to find us. To say nothing of whoever I overheard earlier. I don't believe anyone saw me in the north tower, but you can never be too careful." Roust hurried them along a flickering passageway Jax did not recall seeing during their earlier journey to the west wing.

"Did you hear anything else?" Captain Solomon further pressed as their Courtier marched them along the path.

"Now is not the time, I'm sorry," Roust said in a hissing whisper. "We're too close to the evening's festivities and the prying ears that may be listening. Please, meet me in the library once dinner concludes. One of the guards stationed at the banquet can show you the way. Now, I must go and announce you all." Ignoring their protests, he skittered out of sight.

Perry and George both gave Jax worried glances.

"I hope you realize you are not allowed to leave our sights tonight," George said with brotherly determination. "Not with someone spouting about causing chaos."

"It certainly sounds like someone does not have peace talks quite foremost in their minds," Jax murmured, her dry humor not as appreciated as much as it normally would be in light of the danger they could be walking into.

"Who could it have possibly been?" Perry asked quietly as they reached the grand archway leading into the banquet hall.

Ahead of them, Jax saw Duchess Tandora and her lady-in-waiting speaking to several men, each of whom bore the seal of a High Courtier. From the colors accenting their plain robes, she guessed they were from Hestes, Kwatalar, and Beautraud. Duke Crepsta also waited at the archway with his wife, being next in line to be announced and ushered into the dining room. "It doesn't sound like Roust recognized the voices, which has me worried."

At that moment, she desperately wanted to tell the two of them that she now suspected Duke Lysandeir of using the peace talks as an opportunity to take Cetachi for his own dukedom, but now wasn't the time or place. And yet, if Roust hadn't recognized the voices he'd overheard, Jax feared that this summit might be attacked from multiple fronts.

Clutching the muscular arms of her companions, she pulled them close into her confidences. "See if you can find out who is staying in or around the northern tower. Duke Mensina is in the east wing, so that rules him out, at least for now." She hated suspecting for even a moment that her grandfather might be plotting behind her back.

"I'll stay with Jax if you want to make the rounds, Perry," George suggested. "People here would be more likely to strike up a conversation with you than with me."

Perry nodded in agreement. "No offense, ol' chap, but you're not the best at small talk." He grinned at the Captain before bestowing a quick kiss on Jax's cheek. "I'll try to circle back around dessert and compare notes."

Perry made his entrance, followed by George, then Jax. All eyes fell on her as she floated into the dazzling candlelit room, her golden jewels illuminating her beauty. The pause in conversation allowed her to take stock of the crowd. She watched Roust leave his post at the stewards' balcony from where he had just called out her name, heading toward a group of Courtiers whom were likely escorts to the visiting delegations. Duke Mensina was speaking animatedly to Duke Crepsta and a few High Courtiers, while Duke Lysandeir was at the front of the room, introducing his family to Duchess Tandora and her lady-in-waiting.

Jax spied the Duke's offspring at his side. She had heard stories about the ethereally beautiful triplets, but seeing them in person still left her shocked. She truly hadn't expected them to look so much alike. The two sons, Lawrence and Landon, could not be distinguished from each other from this distance. Their sister, the famous Lysette, whom Jaquobie had so highly recommended, shared their features but had longer hair and wore a lovely gown. They all had their father's flaming red hair, Jax having never seen the seemingly unnatural shade anywhere before in her life. The triplets were taller and more slender than their father, likely inheriting their lithe frames from their deceased mother. Jax remembered with sadness that Duchess Lysandeir had died during childbirth. Bearing one child was dangerous enough in the realm these days, and three at the same time had proved fatal for the young noble-born woman.

Jax caught a glimpse of Jaquobie off to the side of the large room, inching forward to make an introduction between herself and Lysette, but she wanted to avoid that situation for as long as possible, considering what she had just unearthed about the Duke. Unless she had concrete proof, she did not want to go to Jaquobie with her suspicions, as he would likely accuse her of trying to sabotage his recommendation. She quickly diverted her gaze and focused on the others in the room.

Sauntering to stand at her side, Duke Pettraud was the first to approach, reaching for her hand and planting a reverential kiss on one of her ringed fingers. "It is good to see you looking well, Duchess Jacqueline."

It had been years since Jax had seen Duke Pettraud in person, the lapse in time likely causing her to forget how much he and his son favored each other. The Duke's dark curls were laced with gray strands here and there, but overall, he looked incredibly fit and youthful for his sixty-some years. "As do you, Your Excellence," she replied. "I might mistake you for my betrothed's brother if the candlelight was just right."

The debonair man chuckled at her joke, although his jaw seemed stiff at the mention of Perry. "Considering you haven't thrown my son out of the palace yet, I hope he has been behaving himself."

She was well aware that before his stay in Saphire, Perry was somewhat of a black sheep in his family, suffering in silence after his mother's death. While Perry was a skilled fighter and rider like his six older brothers, he also enjoyed the latest fashions and attending the theatre. He was a particularly gifted painter, a talent he'd hidden from his father for fear of punishment. The Duke did not find it suitable for his youngest son to take pleasure in such a delicate activity.

"Lord Pettraud seems to be thriving in the Saphirian court. My people adore him," Jax replied, managing to hide the annoyance she felt at the question. "I trust you had an uneventful journey up the mountain?" she asked, effectively changing the subject.

The Duke grunted. "I wouldn't put it past Lysandeir to have summoned this weather himself. It made for a terrible ride up." Dipping his head closer to Jax, he murmured, "I think Lucien was hoping that some of us wouldn't show up to this summit, and therefore our votes would count as abstentions."

Jax's eyes cast quickly to George, who stood listening from a few steps away, his gaze riveted on her. The faintest of nods conveyed he had caught the Duke's remark. "Have you heard the latest regarding the vote count?" she asked the Duke in a causal but calculated manner.

Pettraud's lavender eyes, so similar in shade to Perry's, filled with heat. "If you are referring to the change in Zaltor's views, then yes, I have." His lips tightened into a thin, nearly imperceptible line. "I've also heard rumors that Beautraud is this close to switching their vote, as well."

Jax grimaced. "What could Lysandeir possibly offer Beautraud that our alliance can't?"

Worry spilled into the Duke's eyes. "Duchess, have you thought about the possibility of Lysandeir organizing some type of coup to overthrow Saphire's influence in the realm?"

"I'd be a fool if I didn't," Jax hissed, detesting that the Duke thought she would be so naïve about her position. "I spend every waking moment wondering which duchy will try to sabotage the prosperity I have nurtured since taking over for my father."

At the mention of his old friend, Perry's father grew quiet. "He would be very proud of you and what you've accomplished so far, my dear. You were the brightest star in his life."

The sincere sentiment took her off guard. "Thank you, Your Excellence." She left it at that, not wanting to think about her father in this tense moment. She was inclined to say more, that Lucien could never hold a candle to Saphire's economy ruling from this snowy tundra, but she reined in her temper. "If you'll excuse me, Duke Pettraud, I've spotted my aunt and I must say hello."

With a parting curtsy, Jax glided over to Lady Annette, who stood in the corner sipping mead from a crystal goblet, her attention elsewhere. As she approached her aunt, Jax, as always, was astounded by the resemblance between Annette and her sister—Jax's departed mother, Amaryllis. Both had the same delicate nose and high cheekbones. Annette even wore her honey-colored hair in a style similar to Jax's mother, whose tresses were the same hue. In a marked difference between the sisters, Annette seemed to have an aura of contentment about her, while Jax's mother had always maintained a mask of cool superiority.

Tonight, Annette looked the part she was meant to play while attending the summit. She easily outshone Duchess Tandora and Duke Crepsta's wife in her fine satin gown. With a small tiara shimmering in her hair, she looked like a Duchess herself.

"Hello, dear aunt. I am so glad to see a friendly face in the crowd," Jax cooed as she reached Annette's side.

Startled from her thoughts, Annette wrapped an arm around her niece. "Goodness, Jacqueline, you gave me a fright. Here I was, thinking I was going to be left to my own devices all evening." She released Jax and took another reassuring sip of her drink. "What delayed you? People were starting to gossip that you would not be attending tonight's dinner."

Cringing, Jax realized Roust's warnings had been right. Every single one of her movements was being watched and analyzed. "You know Perry. He won't leave his room until every last seam is crisp and perfect."

Annette's eyes slid over to her soon-to-be nephew by marriage. "Well, there's not a figure in here more dashing than he, so I suppose it's all worth the wait." She giggled, then motioned to a platter of fruit tarts on display at a nearby table. "You may want to grab some while you can. There's no guessing how long Lysandeir is going to rattle on before allowing us to sit down for dinner."

Jax popped a cherry pastry in her mouth, her stomach grumbling in gratitude. "I pray that he keeps the longwinded speeches for tomorrow, instead of ruining tonight. I think I smell partridge coming from the hall."

Annette laughed once again, impressed by Jax's love of food. "You can always sniff out a good meal," she said lightly before pulling her niece closer. "Father and I are also hopeful that you can unearth Lysandeir's true intentions regarding this whole Cetachi nonsense."

"Dear aunt, I must ask you to keep your voice down," Jax chastised, her eyes scanning their surroundings. She relaxed when she saw there was no one within twenty feet of their little nook. "I'm hoping to gather some more information before the official talks begin tomorrow. Duke Pettraud seems to think Lysandeir is amassing some sort of coup."

Annette's eyes widened. "There would be no hope of that. The wealth of Saphire, Mensina, and Pettraud alone is enough to overshadow the other duchies."

"True," Jax conceded, "but we don't really know the wealth that could be hidden in the wilds of Cetachi. Master Fangard certainly seems to have made a small fortune for himself, just based on his appearance alone." Her eyes caught sight of Darian moving around the room, trying in vain to introduce himself to members of the visiting delegations. She felt a little sorry for him, for most were not giving him the time of day. Even Duchess Tandora, who was supposed to be supporting the Cetachi Accord, hardly acknowledged his presence when he came to speak with her and her lady-in-waiting.

"Have you spent any time with Darian? What do you think of him?" Jax asked her aunt.

Annette's cheeks blossomed red under her makeup. "We had lunch together, and then tea with my father. Such an engaging conversationalist and very brilliant, despite a lack of formal education. I must say, I won't be too disappointed by our change in plans, if you know what I mean." Her lilac eyes, rimmed with the golden hues of her mother's noble bloodline, appraised the young revolutionary's striking profile. "He's so young and hopeful, the poor thing. He thinks that Lysandeir is a champion for his advocating of freedom across Cetachi. Although…" She paused, continuing after a few seconds, "…he was still shaken up about that Maegus fellow being escorted here."

Jax continued to survey the subject of their conversation as he moved around the room. She was pleased to see Perry skillfully intercept the Cetachi statesman and strike up a chat. If anyone could befriend Darian and get information out of him unknowingly, it was Perry. "Did he say why?" she said to her aunt. "You'd think he'd want his right-hand man to be by his side during these talks."

Annette shrugged. "He said tensions were still high after the election. He's worried that his opposition might try something nefarious while he is away from the region."

This presented a new angle for Jax to consider. Darian had indeed been elected governor by his people, but what had become of his opponents in the race? She couldn't imagine they would have accepted defeat lightly. "And he trusted Welles to keep the peace in his stead?" She couldn't help but snort at the idea of the brooding Maegus as peacekeeper.

"Apparently. Maegus was the leader of a nomadic group from the western shores of the region who approached Darian earlier this year. He wanted to back Darian in the upcoming election," Annette divulged.

"He just appeared out of thin air and tossed his support to a baker's son?" Jax shot an incredulous look at her aunt.

"I know it's hard to get news from the Cetachi region that hasn't been muddied with gossip, but this is straight from Darian's lips." Annette's eyes glazed over for a moment, and Jax had to wonder if her aunt was picturing those handsome lips doing more than just talking.

Clearing her throat—perhaps to pull her thoughts away from Darian—Annette continued. "Tomorrow, Father has asked for Darian to recount for the summit leaders how the election unfolded, in the hopes of understanding how these players came into power." She gave Jax a knowing smirk.

"Well, I don't want to wait until tomorrow. I'm going to get it straight from the horse's mouth. Please excuse me." Jax snatched one last cherry tart from the nearby tray before strolling toward Perry and Darian.

"Incoming, Jax." Appearing out of thin air at her shoulder, George's warning whisper barely registered quickly enough for her to prepare for Jaquobie's advances.

"Duchess, might we take this moment to become acquainted with Lady Lysette?" Jaquobie wrapped spindle-like fingers around her arm and led her to the front of the room, where Duke Lysandeir and his children congregated around a massive fireplace.

Jax knew there was no sense in protesting; it would come across as childish, and truthfully, she just wanted this whole charade to be over with. "Where did you disappear to this afternoon?" she asked with a snap as they approached the redheaded group.

"I was taking care of some business," Jaquobie replied rather vaguely, his words making Jax shiver with slight unease. "I'll inform you later."

Then, Jaquobie did something she did not expect. He turned on the charm. Bowing low before Lysette, Jaquobie waved a hand in Jax's direction. "Her Illustrious Highness, Duchess Jacqueline Arienta Xavier has been eager to make your acquaintance, Lady Lysette." He gave the striking young woman a smile that actually reached his eyes.

Jax's gaze flickered from Jaquobie to Lysette for a brief moment, trying to shake off the feeling that these two somehow knew each other. "Lady Lysette. High Courtier Jaquobie has praised many fine things about you. I am delighted to meet you in person." She extended a hand in warm greeting, not bothering with the formal curtsies.

Lysette turned her attention to Jax, a mixture of awe and wariness dancing across her porcelain face. "Duchess Jacqueline, it is I who have heard wonderful tales about you. My brothers and I find your adventurous exploits to be truly entertaining. Why, we recently saw Michelangelo Montivarius's newest show. Lady Giovanna made you come alive onstage!" she trilled with delight.

Jax concealed her embarrassment at being the subject of the renowned playwright's latest production, although she was pleased to be portrayed by the talented actress. "I haven't had the time to see it myself, but I've heard rave reviews about it. Lord Pettraud certainly is eager to see it."

Lysette's head bobbed up and down in a comical manner. "Indeed. I was on the edge of my seat the entire time. I can't believe you lived through it!"

"I'm sure Montivarius took some artistic liberties along the way." Jax could only imagine how the playwright had decided to craft her journey on *Rose of the Sea* the previous spring. "Although I can say I have stayed away from sea travel since sailing back from Isla DeLacqua."

"I'm sure. Goodness, it would take me years to recover from seeing someone murdered!" Lysette's hand flew to her heart.

Well, with my record, my lady-in-waiting needs to have a stronger stomach than that, Jax thought. Amused by her own thoughts, she smiled at Lysette. "I take it you saw the show in Hestes?"

"Oh yes, it's one of my favorite duchies to visit when we're not trapped in this fortress by snow." She demonstrated her displeasure with a slight shudder. "Father enjoys going to Savant, as he spent much of his youth there, but I always try to arrange a stop in Hestes. I am a fan of their vineyards." In an action that Jax found to be rather tacky, Lysette winked.

"Would you introduce me to your brothers?" Jax changed the subject in hopes of expanding her circle of companions. Despite George trailing her like a shadow, he had remained quiet, although his face reflected what he thought of Lysette's birdbrained personality.

"Oh, sure thing!" Lysette whipped her head around and summoned her brothers with a terse exchange of looks. Jax wondered for a moment if the triplets had some uncanny ability to communicate without words.

Leaving their father's side, the identical young men came to flank their sister. With the Lysandeir siblings standing directly in front of her, Jax felt her unease grow stronger. As a united front, their similar appearance was quite unsettling.

Lysette waved a hand first toward the brother on the right, then the left. "This is Lawrence…and Landon."

They bowed in greeting, and Jax forced a smile. "You must get this question all the time, but how in the name of the Virtues are we to tell you apart from one another?"

The boys looked at each other, likely sharing some inside joke. "Why don't you take another look at us, Duchess?" Lawrence—at least she believed it was Lawrence—challenged.

Jax bristled at the dare, but consented. She studied them carefully, feeling no shame in scanning every inch of their appearance. Apparently, they were no strangers to her reputation for solving mysteries; she wanted to prove that her observational skills were indeed real. Her gaze heated as she took in their faces once more.

Frowning, she was just about to accept defeat and ask them again, when a wink from Landon made everything fall into place. "Your eyes!" she said in amazement. "Landon has purple eyes, and Lawrence has amber."

"And you'll also notice I have one of each," Lysette gushed with inflated pride.

Jax returned her gaze to the young woman she'd been conversing with and indeed realized that while one eye was lavender like her father's, the other was amber-colored. "Incredible. I've never seen anything like it before."

"It's a rare occurrence, but it's been known to happen before," tawny-eyed Lawrence explained. "With our mother being noble-born and all."

Now that she saw the difference in their appearances, Jax knew she would always be able to tell them apart. "It must be a nice reminder for your father to see your mother's eyes."

Jax hadn't meant her words to be hurtful, but she immediately saw a tragic reaction to her statement. Landon and Lawrence's expressions hardened and Lysette's eyes rimmed with tears. "Oh Virtues, I meant no offense," she said in dismay, wishing she could retract her words.

Without explanation, Landon and Lawrence dutifully retreated to their father's side. Duke Lysandeir seemed to take notice, as he shot a threatening look in Jax's direction.

"Of course you didn't, Duchess." Lysette collected herself before any tears fell from her eyes. "It's just a sensitive subject."

Jax was no stranger to mourning a mother's absence, but the triplets were only a year or two younger than she and had never known their mother. Why was their grief still so raw?

Jaquobie, who had stepped back a respectful distance while Jax spoke with the siblings, appeared at her side, as if eager to repair the damage she'd done. "Lady Lysette, might I escort you to your seat? It appears we will be sitting down to dine soon." He threw a chastising look at Jax, and she knew she'd hear about this incident later.

"Why, thank you, High Courtier." Lysette curtsied to Jax. "It was a pleasure speaking with you, Your Grace," Lysette said before lacing her arm through Jaquobie's and gliding away from a puzzled Jax.

"Well, that turned sour fast," George murmured as he moved from behind her.

Jax turned to him, her eyebrows raised. "I haven't put my foot in my mouth that badly since my first year at the Academy." She felt a rush of guilt bubbling up inside her. She hadn't been particularly impressed with Lysette, but she certainly hadn't meant to upset her.

"Let's chalk it up to everyone being hungry." George could clearly see she was at war with herself. "Why don't we get our seats, as well?"

Nodding, Jax followed the captain to the dining table that stretched nearly the entire length of the grand banquet room. The high stone walls were void of decoration, a common theme she had noticed throughout the imposing citadel. The real beauty came from massive iron chandeliers dangling from the arched ceiling, long arms supporting nearly a hundred candles per fixture. As she approached the table, she took a moment to admire the rigid exquisiteness of the room. When she entered earlier, she had been too focused on the guests to notice.

The attendees of the summit began to shuffle around, courtiers escorting royalty to their seats and then finding their own. Roust, however, was nowhere to be seen. *I hope he's all right*, Jax thought as she found her seat without assistance. She looked at the placards of her neighbors. Duchess Crepsta was to her left, which Jax was perfectly fine with. She got along well with the Duke's wife; she enjoyed her desserts nearly as much as Jax did.

As Jax looked at the name card to her right, her heart sank. Maegus Welles. She doubted the brooding man would be an enjoyable dinner companion, but it might be a good opportunity to try and coax some information out of him. As to why Duke Lysandeir personally rode out to bring the Warden to the summit, she still had no idea.

Duchess Crepsta reached the table shortly after Jax, thanking her courtier and kissing Jax warmly on both cheeks. "Duchess, it is wonderful to be in your company. Did you get a chance to try the peach tarts they were passing around?" The refined woman discreetly raised her chin in the direction of the hors d'oeuvre trays the servants were now carrying out of the room as they prepared to serve the main meal.

Jax grinned. "I went for the cherry ones. Now that I've gotten my serving of fruit out of the way, I can ask the Virtues for a chocolate-themed dessert."

A hopeful grin slid across Duchess Crepsta's features. "I've been praying for something dripping in caramel, myself. We'll soon see which of us the Virtues favor," she said with a giggle before turning to her neighbor, a High Courtier from Kwatalar, to make the proper introductions.

"I'm surprised that captain of yours hasn't searched me over for any daggers I might be hiding up my sleeves," sounded a gravel-laced voice from behind Jax.

Her head snapped to attention. She turned to see Maegus Welles place a weathered hand on the back of his chair, sliding it out from under the table. "I'm sure that could be arranged. Should I call him over?" One eyebrow cocked as she issued the challenge.

"No need, Your Grace. I would not dream of marring such breathtaking beauty," Maegus said with a snicker, his gruff exterior cracking ever so slightly.

"I'm amazed you're being forced to sit beside the likes of me. From what I've heard, you're extremely close to our host." Jax's eyes slid to the head of the table where Lucien sat conversing with Darian, seated to his left as the guest of honor. "Shouldn't a Warden be with his governor?"

Maegus picked up his napkin and placed it over his lap. "Scoff as much as you'd like about our plans, Duchess, but Darian's vision will lead Cetachi to a bright future."

Jax pressed her lips together. It may lead them there, but what exactly did that future hold?

"I take it from your silence that you are astonished by my knowledge of ducal table etiquette," Maegus said with a slightly teasing tone.

Although Jax hadn't even taken notice, she allowed herself to be baited. "Where did you learn such graces in the wilds of Cetachi?" She smirked with unveiled condescension.

Maegus grunted. "I am the leader of the western region, Your Grace."

"A *tribe* in the western region, I heard." Now Jax provided the bait, hoping to learn more.

"The way you say 'tribe' makes me think you believe we live in huts and tents. I think you'd find that our 'tribes' are just as civilized as your villages and cities. Our architecture might not be quite as advanced, but we certainly are able to put secure roofs over our peoples' heads."

That tidbit of information did surprise Jax. From the tales she'd heard throughout her whole life, she pictured nomadic people roaming across Cetachi, having no place to call home. "And how does a leader of a tribe come to be the first elected Warden?"

"Once I heard the work Darian was doing to help people in his own tribe, I knew he was a leader the whole nation could flourish under. So, I set out to meet him. He talked about his plans for all of five minutes before I dedicated myself to his cause."

Jax paused to watch Duke Lysandeir rise from his seat, the simple action bringing the room to silence. As much as she wanted to learn more about Maegus and Darian's rise to power, she had to turn her attentions to their smirking host.

"Greetings, sovereigns of the realm! It is an honor to host such a monumental summit. Not since the Rebirth has such progressive change been thrust upon this land. For centuries, our neighbors in

Cetachi have struggled, their people suffering while their land remained fractured and split. Now, we have the chance to offer salvation at the hands of Darian Fangard, the first elected official in the Realm of Virtues, whether some of you recognize him or not." Lysandeir paused, not bothering to hide blatant stares at those who opposed the Accord. "But let us put aside our differences tonight and enjoy the grand company around our table. To the Virtues!" He raised a silver goblet high, watching like a hawk to see that everyone followed suit.

Jax delicately sipped her mead, promising herself no more would pass her lips for the rest of the evening. She needed her mind to be sharp as ever if she was going to unearth any foul plots. "I almost wished your Darian was the one giving tonight's toast. I'm sure it would have been more well-spoken than that." Jax risked a jab at Lysandeir to see Maegus's reaction.

His face, however, remained stony and unyielding. "Darian has been blessed by the Virtues to receive such staunch support from Duke Lysandeir."

"The fact that Cetachi raids have been terrorizing his duchy for decades doesn't have anything to do with it?" Jax asked, her words clipped and pointed.

"Darian put an end to the raids as soon as he was elected. That was months before Lysandeir approached him with the offer to support his claim for statehood." A note of pride crept into Maegus's reply.

Jax resisted a triumphant smile as she stewed over the information. So, Lysandeir was indeed the one to put the pieces into motion regarding Cetachi's formal position in the realm. Maegus clearly didn't understand the prize he had let slip, for he busied himself eating his salad as if nothing was amiss. As much as she wanted to ask him right here and now, Jax withheld her question. She would ask Darian himself if plans to become recognized by the duchies had been on his mind before Lysandeir entered the picture.

"I understand that we almost didn't have the pleasure of your company," Jax asked with mock regret as she tore apart a butter-drenched roll.

Maegus scowled. "My, word travels around here fast."

Jax studied his face as he put his thoughts together, waiting for his response.

"Once Duke Lysandeir found out Darian was traveling alone, he sent for me to accompany the Governor, in case he needed my support during the summit," Maegus nonchalantly explained.

"Being sent for is quite different than the Duke riding out to meet you himself," Jax pointed out.

The Warden's voice held a hint of annoyance, as though he was beginning to tire of Jax's peppering questions. "As I said before, Darian has been blessed to receive Lysandeir's support through this entire matter."

"It sure does seem that way," Jax answered as she thoughtfully chewed on lemon oil-seasoned salad.

Without another word, Maegus turned his attention to the Kwatalar courtiers on his right, ignoring any further questions Jax may have wanted to ask.

For the rest of the meal, she dabbled in conversations with Duchess Crepsta and the High Courtiers sitting across from her, although the table was so wide, it was hard to keep steady chatter with those on the other side. In absence of conversation, she busied herself with her roasted partridge, grilled asparagus, and glazed potatoes. As much as she wanted to find fault with Lysandeir, the palace cook was indeed talented.

Placing her fork down on her empty dessert plate, Jax swiped her napkin across her lips for any remnants of chocolate soufflé, determined not to leave so much as a morsel behind. She watched Perry and Annette, seated toward the opposite end of the table from Lysandeir, in animated conversation with a few of the Mensina courtiers. Her grandfather, a few seats up to her left, was chatting with Landon and Duke Crepsta. She recalled that Landon was the firstborn of the triplets, and, with his wholly lavender eyes, would inherit the throne one day from his father.

Her gaze landed last on Darian, who appeared to be staring off at nothing. In a booming voice, Lysandeir told the guests sitting closest to him of some hunting tale, but Darian seemed completely disinterested in the conversation. She saw a deepening sadness in his eyes as his thoughts seemed to drift further and further away from the goings-on at the table.

"Likely thinking about his father." Maegus, apparently having noticed her staring, broke into her thoughts. "There's nothing more that young man wants than to build a Cetachi where hardworking people like his father don't have to suffer in silence."

Maegus's claims haunted Jax as everyone began to disperse for the night. In order to bring Darian to their side, she had to be able to convince him that his people wouldn't suffer under a dukedom. *It shouldn't be hard*, she thought. *My people are happy and well-cared for.* But she couldn't help but remember the venom in Hendrie's eyes. Was she so blind to suffering that she did not see? Her appointed courtiers were meant to report on the well-being of her people. She couldn't very well be everywhere at once. She trusted them to inform her of any problems. Perhaps there were things that had gotten lost along the way.

"Jax, everything all right?" Perry whispered as he reached her side to escort her out of the banquet room. "You look a bit dazed."

"I'm fine," she said, chiding herself for being so transparent. "I have a lot on my mind, that's all." She doubted she fooled Perry, but if he knew she was hiding something from him, he didn't press the matter.

"Shall we go find Sir Roust?" he suggested.

Jax had almost forgotten about their plans to meet the courtier in the library. "Yes, let's see what secrets he's keeping."

Chapter Nine

George joined them a moment later, shirking away from the swooning clutches of Duchess Tandora's lady-in-waiting. "Lady Gwendolyn was quite attentive this evening," he said with a beet-red glower as Jax and Perry chuckled at the woman's acid expression as she headed back to her room alone.

"Is she new to the post? I don't remember seeing her at the Duchess's side before," Jax asked once her giggles subsided.

George nodded. "She's only been in her service for a few months. The previous lady-in-waiting married a Tandorian Earl and moved to his estate. Lady Gwen's father is a close family friend of the Duchess. I guess she'd been preparing for the position for quite some time."

Jax regarded the woman's retreating figure. "Well, she's not half bad looking, George. I'd excuse you for the night if you're interested."

George rolled his eyes as Jax and Perry dissolved into fits of laughter once more. "Come on, you two. Let's find a guard to take us to the library." He didn't even deem their joke worthy of a response.

After encountering a guard who protested that guests should return to their rooms, Captain Solomon was able to persuade him that the Duchess simply wanted some reading material and hadn't packed any. A few moments later, the group arrived at two huge metal doors, illuminated by enormous torches.

"Would you like me to wait to escort you back to your rooms?" The guard must have noticed their designated courtier was not present.

"No need," George said without further explanation.

Giving them another inquisitive glance, the guard took his leave and disappeared down the hall.

"I hope he's not running right to Lysandeir to tell him where we are," Jax said, looking apprehensive as the guardsman retreated. "He'll know something is up if we're reported skirting around the archives, and I don't want Roust being found out. He's in a dangerous position."

"Well, let's hope the information he has is worth the trouble." With a grunt, Perry pushed open the heavy doors to the library, George jumping into help.

Despite the late hour, the cavernous room glowed with warmth, several fireplaces lining the walls. The endless rows of shelves seemed to reach the ceiling, ladders perched against the hardwood to allow patrons access to the high-placed volumes. The smell of books filled their noses as they entered the vault of knowledge.

Jax saw a few scholars still scribbling away furiously, the candles at their worktables nearly melted down to stubs. "Let's find Roust."

The rotund, bleary-eyed courtier was tucked away in a section labeled *Prose*. "Thank the Virtues you made it. I was beginning to worry you might not come." He ushered them to a small table, away from prying eyes. "Don't worry, no one will ever suspect me of hiding out among works of fiction." He tittered at his own joke.

"Enough small talk. Is there a threat to the Duchess's life that you know about?" George demanded, his patience for the evening at its end.

Roust wiped a bead of sweat off his balding head. "No, no, I suspect nothing of that. But I do believe the duchies have been lured here under false pretenses." He looked at Jax, then at Perry, and then back at George. "I prepared a few of the invitations that were sent to the leaders. Their wording made it seem that Cetachi was the one forcing the realm's hand to accept it as a state. But from the whisperings I've overheard, the Duke is the one behind the charge."

While Perry and George looked surprised at this revelation, for Jax it merely affirmed what Maegus and her grandfather had shared earlier. "So, it is true then. Lysandeir was the one who approached Darian to legitimize his newly formed government," she said in dark wonder.

"I think he did more than just approach." Roust raised his eyebrows.

"Did he threaten Darian?" Jax found it hard to believe someone as idealistic as the Governor appeared to be could be so easily swayed.

Roust shook his head. "This is where I need your help, Duchess. I don't have any proof that Lysandeir is strong-arming Cetachi. But there have been too many gossiping whispers floating about the castle since these peace talks were announced for there not to be something more cunning afoot."

"What else have you heard to make you think so?" Perry asked, confusion written all over his face.

"Lysandeir has made many trips to Cetachi over the past few weeks. He's hardly back two days before he sets out again. But when he finally greeted Darian after the young man's arrival, Darian said, and I quote, 'It's good to see you, Lucien. It's been a few *months* since our paths crossed.'" Roust paused for dramatic effect, allowing the information to seep in.

This caused a reshuffling of Jax's thoughts. "And you're sure the Duke has been going to Cetachi during these visits? He's not just covering up a romantic tryst that he wants kept secret or something like that?" she inquired, knowing that Dukes and Duchesses alike often arranged alternative plans to cover up their indiscretions.

"I've recently befriended one of the Duke's personal guardsmen," Roust replied. "He has verified the Duke's visits to Cetachi. He says they always go to a small outpost near our eastern borders. The Duke holds a few closed-door meetings, then returns." As if anticipating Jax's next question, he added, "My contact has never seen who the Duke meets with. Lysandeir orders his men to wait outside the encampment."

George's eyes widened in disbelief. "And the Captain of the Ducal Guard allowed this?"

Roust nodded. "My friend said the last Captain was discharged because he protested too much. This new one seems to know better than to disobey Lysandeir's orders."

Jax exchanged glances with her captain. She knew George would fight tooth and nail should she ever demand to go into an enemy encampment alone. "So, all we know for certain is that Lysandeir is having secret meetings with someone in Cetachi. How long has this been going on?"

Roust thought for a few moments. "I guess I never really took notice until seeing the invitations a little more than two months ago. But by then, Lysandeir had already been to Cetachi a handful of times and continued the frequent visits."

"Would your guard friend be willing to testify as to Lysandeir's trips to Cetachi?" Jax asked. "I'm sure this would be enough for the summit to put the Accord on hold, especially if he's not meeting with Darian."

Roust shook his head. "I'm afraid the young man is too fearful of what the Duke might do to him or his family should he speak up."

Jax gritted her teeth in frustration. "I'll have to see if I can trick it out of Lucien during the peace talks tomorrow."

"What about what Roust overheard in the tower, about chaos being unleashed?" Perry pointed out another piece of the puzzle. "I asked around, and both the Tandora and Crepsta delegations are staying in the north tower."

"Tandora is voting for the Accord. Perhaps the Duchess is a part of Lysandeir's plot. Could she be the one you overheard, Roust?" Jax looked intently at the stout man.

More sweat appeared above his brow. "I really don't know, Duchess. The voices were so muffled, I couldn't tell if they were coming from men or women."

"It could also be someone plotting against Lysandeir," Perry mused. "Do you think Crepsta would take matters into his own hands without telling us?"

"After what his nephew did to my parents, there is nothing Crepsta does that I don't know about," Jax said with vehemence. "He's not someone we have to worry about."

"What about Duke Pettraud?" George posed the question they all had been thinking. "Can we trust him not to act irrationally against Lysandeir?"

Jax reluctantly looked into Perry's worried eyes. "I want to trust him, I do," she said, speaking from her heart. "But he is well aware of the deal that Zaltor made with Lucien. If he thinks Beautraud might also defect, he might be willing to take some risks, especially with his son about to marry the Saphire throne." Her cheeks reddened as her words trailed off, embarrassed how easily the scenario formed in her mind.

"I could try to talk to him, see what he knows," Perry suggested. "Since I'm the disappointment-turned-prodigal son, he might be willing to share a few secrets with me."

Jax saw a fountain of hesitation trickling behind his eyes. She smiled and squeezed his hand. "Good idea. I'll send Jaquobie tomorrow morning to set something up. In the meantime, all we know is that someone is planning something, which is not a lot to go on, to say the least." Her expression grim, she added, "Everyone, be alert and traverse the castle with care. You, especially, Roust." Her gaze focused on the trembling man. "I'd like you to stay in the Saphire apartments where my guards can watch your back. If anyone asks why, just tell them I want you at my beck and call. That sounds like something I'd demand." She resisted a wry smile. "George, can you make sure he has a bed?"

"There's a spare cot in my room." George nodded. "You're welcome to it, Roust. Do you need to fetch anything from your quarters?"

The courtier looked as if he might burst into tears. Clearly, the intensity of the situation was becoming too much for him. "I do have a few things I'd like to bring along, if you don't mind."

"Of course not," Jax answered. "Captain Solomon will escort you to collect your things and bring them to the west wing. Lord Pettraud and I will find a guard to lead us back if we get lost."

George looked sternly at her. "I don't think I should leave you unattended either, Duchess."

Perry nudged the Captain's arm. "What am I? Another pretty face? I can see her safely up a few flights of stairs." His tone was light and joking, but Jax detected a hint of annoyance.

George must have noticed it, too, for he conceded. "I'll let you know once the Courtier is safely ensconced in my room." He motioned Roust to follow, and the two cautiously slinked out of the library.

"Ah, finally. I thought they'd never leave," Perry teased just before his lips pecked Jax on the cheek.

"You're incorrigible." Jax laughed, pushing him away as he leaned in for another kiss. "Not here, you buffoon." She gathered her skirts and started for the exit. As much as she was tempted to enjoy Perry's company, she knew better than to fawn over him in view of a room full of foreign scholars. "Perhaps we can take a short, romantic detour during our walk back," she cooed with a wink, waiting while her future Prince Consort struggled to open the metal door.

A bit winded, Perry glanced behind them as they walked down the dark passage, hands entwined. "Doesn't look like Lysandeir wants the library to be a place of easy access. I wonder what he's hiding?"

"Or maybe he's trying to keep the scholars stuck inside to prevent them from poking around into other affairs of the castle," Jax murmured, thinking about Roust and his claims. "I do hope my court keeps its secrets better than Lucien's does."

"You do feel safe with me, don't you, Jax? You know I will do anything to protect you."

Caught off guard by the question, she swiftly turned her head to meet his gaze, stunned by his bashful expression. "Of course, Perry." She stroked his cheek with affection. "You know how dedicated George is. He was simply doing his job."

He sighed, looking rather defeated. "It's just...I want to be so much more than an accessory on your arm. I want to help you. I want to help Saphire. I want our marriage to be a partnership, not something where I'm just sent to play in the corner and paint."

Jax studied him for a moment, wondering where all this was coming from. Had seeing his father again caused his insecurities to resurface? "I want that, too, Perry. That's why you'll be with me during the Accord tomorrow. I want us to present a united front...even if we do not necessarily agree with everything the other does."

Perry's eyes narrowed. "Are you referring to the opinions Hendrie and I shared about allowing people to elect their own leaders?"

She blushed. "Maybe."

"I said I would tow the Saphire line, Jax. Although, after the insanity we've seen from Lysandeir today, I'm not sure you have a leg to stand on." As he spoke, anger at the Duke's disregard for his position blossomed across his face.

Jax had been steeling herself for that comment all day, but before she could mount her defense, something up ahead caught her attention. Gripping Perry's arm, Jax forced him to focus on the looming staircase that would take them back to the west wing. "What's that at the bottom of the steps, Perry?" Her voice came out as a strained whisper.

Alone in the hallway, the pair inched closer, the flickering torchlight deceptively concealing what lay ahead on the stone floor. They were only a few feet away when Jax's hand flew to her mouth in horror. "Annette?"

Breaking away from Perry's side, Jax dashed forward, kneeling beside the woman's crumpled body. She quickly saw that the blond tresses were a few shades too light to be Annette's, but her relief was short lived. Rolling the woman over in a frantic search for a pulse, Jax's blood ran cold.

The bulging eyes of Duchess Tandora's lady-in-waiting stared at her lifelessly.

Chapter Ten

"Virtues sake, Jax, what do you think happened?" Perry was at her side a moment later, his skin tinged with an uneasy green hue. "Did she fall down the stairs?"

Jax wished daylight streamed through the windows so she could search the surrounding area more thoroughly. "I highly doubt it." She motioned for him to look at the woman's broken neck. "Even in this light, I can see the beginnings of some bruising. I'd be willing to bet she was strangled, then pushed."

"Poor girl." Perry pressed a handkerchief to his mouth, not used to seeing death up this close. "What was she doing down here? The Tandora delegation is in the north wing."

"Perhaps she was on her way to visit a specific Saphirian captain for an impromptu night cap," Jax theorized with grim humor.

"George is going to be horrified that she was assaulted seeking him out."

"Run and find the guards, Perry. They'll be able to alert Lysandeir and his court physician." Jax waved him away. "I'll be fine with her here. I think our culprit is long gone."

Perry hesitated, looking uncertain about leaving her alone, but ultimately did as she instructed. Watching his figure retreat down the hall for a moment, Jax turned her attention back to the deceased Lady Gwendolyn. Acting quickly, she jumped to her feet and pulled one of the torches from the wall, bringing the flame closer for proper examination.

Indeed, there was bruising around the woman's neck, the outline of hands becoming more prominent with each passing moment. Her skin wasn't cool to the touch, but it wasn't warm, either. Jax guessed she could have been lying out here since the feast ended. They'd been speaking with Roust for well over an hour, so the timeline added up.

Her jewelry was still intact, so the deceased hadn't been robbed. Looking at the signet on her finger that indicated her position as lady-in-waiting, Jax noticed the woman's hand clasped a bit of paper. Carefully pulling the parchment away from stiff fingers, Jax opened the note.

Meet me soon. G.S.

Rage ripped through her. The handwriting on the note was nowhere near comparable to George's own hand. This poor woman had been falsely lured out of her room and sent to her death.

She heard shouts and shuffling emerge from down the hall, Perry no doubt having alerted the castle about the incident. As the first guards reached Jax and asked her to step away, all the Duchess could think about in the darkness was why the woman had been targeted.

‡

"I still think you should have shown the guards that note, Jax," Perry reprimanded her—and not for the first time—as they finally reached the door to her suite. "They could see if they could match the handwriting to any of the palace guests."

Jax gave him a severe look. "Perry, you saw Lysandeir's face. He's going to try and cover this up, make it out to be an accident. If I gave his guards the note, I'm sure it would get tossed into the fire." She paused, letting a sly smile slip across her lips. "And besides, *I* plan to be the one to match the handwriting."

Perry threw his arms up in the air. "We've got enough to worry about regarding Cetachi and Lysandeir. We don't need to add investigating that poor woman's death to the pile."

Jax grasped Perry's arm, beseeching him to see the entire picture as she pulled him into the privacy of her chambers. "Roust overheard that someone is planning to cause chaos during the summit. I can't think of anything that would plunge a castle into chaos better than the murder of a young, attractive woman."

"But you said Lysandeir plans to cover this up as an accident," Perry sputtered.

Jax decided that the shock of stumbling upon Lady Gwendolyn's twisted figure must have slowed down his mental faculties. "I don't believe that Lysandeir was privy to what Roust overheard in the north tower," she said aloud.

"So, who do you suspect is behind it?"

Jax's shoulders felt heavy. "I don't know at this moment. But I'm sure whoever authored this note will help shed some light on the matter."

A knock on her apartment door signaled the arrival of George and Roust, who entered the room, winded from their lengthy climb.

"Duchess! We heard there'd been an accident," George said between panting breaths, a shaken-looking Roust at his side. "We ran into a wall of guards at the bottom of the stairs, shooing us up to our rooms. What's going on?"

"You'd better sit down," Jax commented dryly, inviting them to take a seat around the fireplace.

Rushing from her adjoining chamber, Uma greeted them. "I was beginning to think you would be out all night." Her eyes widened as the warm, cozy space filled up with guests. "What's going on?"

Jax gestured for her to take a seat as well before divulging what she and Perry had come across during their journey back to the west wing.

George sat in his chair with his head in his hands as she read the note aloud, passing it around for the others to see. No one recognized the writing.

"Oh goodness! Perhaps if I'd gone to the guards with what I overheard, this wouldn't have happened," Roust fretted, dabbling his eyes.

"Or it could have been *you* at the bottom of those stairs," Jax snapped. "What happened to Lady Gwendolyn is devastating, but it goes to prove that we are dealing with an evil force. We must all be on alert." She met each of their gazes with grim determination. "Who would have thought peace talks would begin with murder?"

‡

Commanding the attention of the entire hall, Duke Lysandeir began to speak. "It is with great sadness that I must share some tragic news. Young Lady Gwendolyn from the Tandorian delegation passed away last night." He paused while the room buzzed with murmurs of surprise among the guests. "My court physician has determined she died of a broken neck from a fall down the stairs. My family offers Duchess Tandora our deepest sympathies, and urge the rest of our guests to be careful navigating the unfamiliar passages of this citadel." The Duke's announcement ended on a rather threatening note, a myriad of startled glances shooting around the banquet table the following morning at breakfast.

Jax watched Duchess Tandora throughout the Duke's speech, making careful note that while the Duchess appeared withdrawn, she looked neither sad nor sorry at the sudden, unexpected passing of her lady-in-waiting. In fact, it looked like she hardly cared.

"Blast it, you were right," Perry rasped under his breath from his seat beside her. "Lucien's covering up that Lady Gwen was attacked."

Jax held back her I-told-you-so look and took a bite of the flaky pastry before her. "Even if the cause of death was a broken neck, there's no way a court physician could overlook those handprints on her skin." She seethed as she picked at the remains of her apple strudel. "He's put everyone in danger by pretending there isn't a murderer in our midst."

"Should I tell my father what we suspect? Jaquobie arranged for us to meet when the summit breaks for lunch."

"Warn him that we suspect foul play, but don't go too far into the details," Jax instructed.

Perry gave her an incredulous look. "Do you honestly think he could be behind this, Jax?"

"Do you?" She hated to make Perry think so poorly of his father, but she wasn't sure she could trust anyone outside her inner circle.

Perry wore a conflicted expression, his answer lost on his lips.

"I'm going to have a word with my grandfather and warn him to be careful, too." Jax placed her napkin on the table and pushed her chair away. "But first, I need to run back up to my room to grab the note I found. I want to have it handy in case an opportunity to do some investigating rises."

Perry promptly pushed back his chair and stood. "I'll come with you."

Jax sighed. "It's a straight shoot from here. Did you see how many guards Lysandeir has patrolling the hallways this morning? He knows it's not safe, even if he won't admit it to his guests. I'll be fine for a quick moment."

Perry rolled his eyes. "George would throttle me if I left you alone for even a second, Jax. I bet Gwendolyn thought it was perfectly safe to take a stroll, too, and look what happened to her."

She knew arguing any further would be a lost cause. "All right, come on." She took his hand in hers, hoping that to anyone watching it looked like they were simply sneaking away for a romantic rendezvous.

With haste, they dashed out of the banquet room, leaving behind the sounds of clattering silverware. After the Duke's announcement, all small talk had died out, leaving everyone to their own macabre thoughts.

"Did you happen to catch a glance at Duchess Tandora's reaction to the news?" Jax asked once they arrived at her suite in western tower.

"I was more focused on the Cetachi delegation. Darian looked stunned, but Maegus almost looked bored."

Grabbing the incriminating parchment from her bedside table, Jax tucked the note safely into the pocket of her dark blue skirt. "What would either of them hope to gain by strangling that woman?" she asked as she locked her apartment door behind her. "You'd think that out of everyone here, they'd want these talks to go the smoothest. Having someone die would be most inconvenient to their goals."

"Perhaps we're not dealing with a sound mind," Perry offered as they made their way down the long west wing staircase. "When has any death we've investigated resulted in a culprit who wasn't deranged?"

Jax fought to suppress an inappropriately-timed snort. "I suppose you are right in that regard."

A sneer came from the shadows, startling them both. "Well, once again, you two are seen wandering the corridors, looking like you're up to something."

The sunlight filtering in from the high arching windows danced across Duke Lysandeir's fiery red hair as he sauntered toward them.

Perry bristled under the man's condescending gaze. "Are you following us?"

"You must admit, it did look a little suspicious, you two dashing off together as soon as I announced Lady Gwen's passing," the Duke answered with a noncommittal shrug. "I had to see what caused such an abrupt departure."

"Shouldn't you be attending to your guests, Lucien?" Jax did little to mask the disdain in her voice. She had never thought very highly of Lysandeir before this trip, and now, after all she'd learned, she had the lowest opinion of the power-hungry Duke.

"They are all being escorted to the throne room for the beginning of our peace talks," he replied, clasping his hands behind his back. His eyes darted between the couple, suspicion continuing to glimmer. "Might I ask why you hurried away so quickly from the breakfast table this morning?"

"Might I ask why you failed to announce that Lady Gwendolyn was strangled to death?" Jax countered. "The other guests deserve to know there is a murderer running around this iceberg."

Lucien gave her a tight smile. "I assure you, my court physician declared that the poor woman simply broke her neck in a fall."

"You may want to get a second opinion," Perry drawled.

"I saw the bruising on her neck. I know those were handprints," Jax said, daring the Duke to contradict her.

Breaking away from her gaze, Lucien paced around them, his footsteps rattling throughout the passageway. "That is mere speculation by someone who thinks they have a knack for solving puzzles. And isn't it odd, Duchess, that the moment you arrive in my duchy someone winds up dead?"

Jax's eyes widened at the insult. "I hope you're not suggesting I had anything to do with it."

Lucien's chest swelled with vigor. "I'm just saying that it would be very easy to persuade our guests into thinking that you killed Lady Gwendolyn to frighten Tandora into joining your side of the Accord. You, who have had enough brushes with death to know how to kill someone."

"This is absurd," Perry interrupted, looking like he wanted to punch Lucien in the face. "Duchess Jacqueline was with me the entire time leading up to our discovery of the body."

"Hmm, her loyal fiancé is her only concrete alibi. Or perhaps the one who does her dirty work for her?" The Duke stoked his chin in feigned thought. "I'm merely sharing one version of events that could be perceived…should word get out about the woman's death being anything other than an unfortunate accident."

"Are you threatening us?" Jax stepped forward, closing the distance between them and facing the Duke unafraid. "Because people who get in the way of my trying to find the truth usually don't fare well."

"I want these discussions to go as smoothly as possible, Duchess," Lucien replied with clipped efficiency. "If you want to investigate Lady Gwendolyn's death I can't stop you, but do not let it ruin Cetachi's chance at presenting their case for statehood."

She was almost tempted to ask him what his true intentions were regarding the Cetachi Accord, but she decided to choose her battles with more care. "We will be discreet, Duke."

Sizing the two of them up one last time, he gave a satisfied nod. "Then I shall see you in the throne room in ten minutes." With that, he turned on his heel and stalked down the winding passage.

The couple held their tongues until his echoing footsteps died out. "Can you believe the audacity of that man, to accuse me of murder?" Jax whirled on Perry, her eyes blazing with fury.

He folded his arms across his heaving chest. "Trying to frame you for his deeds is more like it."

Jax sputtered dismissively. "No, as tasteless as that little stunt was, I do not think he sent Lady Gwendolyn to her death. He needs these peace talks to go in his favor. If anything, this has thrown a wrench in his plans." She gathered up her long skirts and began hurrying down the hall. "I want to speak to Duchess Tandora before the summit starts. I need to find out where she stands after all this."

Perry quickened his steps to keep pace with her. "Are you going to tell her that Lady Gwendolyn was attacked?"

Jax considered for only a moment. "I told Duke Lysandeir I would be discreet in my investigation. I'll do so for the time being, but I'm worried our killer isn't done with their chaotic reign."

Chapter Eleven

Jax and Perry, with the assistance of the hallway guards, found their way into the throne room with a few minutes to spare before the summit's official start. Overnight, an oval table had been set up in the middle of the space, roomy enough for all the delegations to congregate around in the high-backed chairs.

Scanning the vast hall for her target, Jax found Duchess Tandora alone, gazing out one of the far windows, her courtiers huddled a few feet away from her. Placing her palm on Perry's chest, she said, "Let me speak with her alone. You can keep an eye on me from the table. I'll be fine." The look of warning in her eyes told him not to object, for she was not pleased about the constant babysitting coming from both her fiancé and the Captain of her Ducal Guard.

Without protest, Perry strolled over to the table to bid Duke Mensina and Annette a good morning.

Jax walked calmly over to Tandora's aging ruler, appraising the woman as she drew closer. While she had not displayed any remorse or sadness at breakfast, Jax could see worry etched all over Delphinia's rough face.

"Duchess, how are you holding up?" Jax asked in a demure tone, bowing her head in greeting to her elder.

"Still in shock, I think," the old woman huffed. "Gwen wasn't in my service for very long, but she was really a lovely girl."

"I am so sorry for your loss. What a terrible thing to befall her." Jax's words rang with sincere sympathy. "Have you sent word to her family?"

The Duchess shook her head. "No, I'd rather speak to her father myself when I return from this cursed summit."

The venom in her words surprised Jax. "Such news is never easy to deliver."

The Duchess's milky eyes narrowed. "Don't pretend that you and I are on the same side, Jacqueline. I still plan to support Cetachi in their claims for statehood."

"Why, if you don't mind me asking? I didn't think an established matriarch like yourself would be a bleeding heart for the democratic cause."

"I could care less about how they manage to rule themselves," Delphinia replied. "As long as the trade agreement Lucien promised me holds, they could worship a pig for all I care."

"What trade agreement? With Cetachi?" Jax's temper began to flare. "Since when does Lucien have the power to arrange that?"

Delphinia's chest rose with regal poise. "Our lush rainforests are drying up. I want to harvest the woodlands along our shared border, so that I can protect what remaining acreage I have near Tafreeni."

"And Lucien promised those trees to you?" Jax's eyebrows rose. "Are those lands really his to give?"

"Governor Fangard was supportive of the measure; he already signed the agreement Lucien delivered to me. Apparently, he, too, believes in the conservation of the rare rainforests my people treasure," the Tandorian replied.

Jax found her opinion of the woman diminishing as their conversation continued. "Ah yes, you treasure them so much, you've nearly leveled them to the ground," she said in a knowing manner. "But why bargain with Cetachi? Pettraud and Mensina have a myriad of woodlands that could be outsourced to your duchy."

"But at what cost?" Delphinia snapped. "The only price I pay with Cetachi is the cost of a vote."

Jax decided she'd had enough. "Glad to see your priorities are sorted out," she tossed over her shoulder as she departed. In a fuming march, she dropped herself into a seat between her grandfather and Perry.

"Learn anything of interest?" Perry asked as he assessed her scowl.

"Only what Delphinia was promised in exchange for her vote. Free wood from Cetachi." Jax crossed her arms, glaring at the empty seats across the table.

"Did she say anything about her lady-in-waiting?" Perry inquired under his breath.

"Well, Gwen had not been in her service for long." Jax sighed. "Although, I did see some genuine distress at her death, so she's not totally immune to it."

"But she doesn't suspect foul play?" Perry prodded.

Shaking her head, Jax looked around the massive table as High Courtiers and leaders alike took their seats. "No, but I believe she does feel guilty about the whole incident."

"Perhaps because she's the reason the poor woman was here in the palace to begin with," Perry mused, but Jax was no longer listening.

Taking his seat across the table, Jaquobie caught her eye for the first time that morning. She was somewhat surprised that her opinionated High Courtier had practically been a ghost ever since their arrival. She mouthed *good morning*, and he responded with a grim smile. Apparently, he no more looked forward to the session ahead than she did.

Duke Lysandeir entered the throne room with his three children, their faces calculating masks of calm. The triplets all sat next to each other, barely making eye contact with anyone else at the table. Lucien, on the other hand, strode around the assembled politicians in a circle, looking triumphant that the summit was about to commence.

"Today will be recounted throughout the realm and written in our histories," he began with honed eloquence. "Cetachi, the wild region to the north, never before able to pull itself out of chaos, stands on the cusp of statehood this very day. Those before me will have the power to change the lives of an entire nation, of the entire realm."

For better or for worse, I wonder, Jax mused.

"Friends and colleagues, I applaud you to listen to reason, which is why I have invited the newly elected Governor of Cetachi to speak a few inspiring words." With a flourish, Duke Lysandeir beckoned the hesitant young statesman to stand before the attentive group.

Jax analyzed Darian with renewed curiosity. She saw fear mingling in his brown eyes, his red cheeks blotchy with nerves. But she also detected his simmering ambition and conviction for what he believed in. It made for an interesting mask on his smooth face.

"Thank you, Your Excellence. It is a great honor to speak before this noble assembly today. Now, I know many of you around the table question my intentions as leader of Cetachi, and you have every right to." Darian looked at the large group of representatives before him. "Cetachi has been secluded in the wilds for so long, it is merely a myth to many people of the realm. But I can tell you that my Cetachi, the Cetachi I have dedicated my life to, is full of compassionate, motivated people who want the chance to live lives full of opportunity…lives where no prospect is denied them, just because they are common-born. I know many of you have your doubts that our people are wise enough to choose a leader who will be good and just for them. But I urge you to look at my sincere character and know I would never do anything to jeopardize their freedoms, nor the trust they have put in me to deliver them a nation unto themselves." His voice broke with emotion, causing him to falter for just a moment. "Thank you."

His declarations were met with silence, but Jax could tell from the expressions of those near her that they had been moved by his passionate words. The High Courtiers from Zaltor and Beautraud made eye contact with slight smiles, and even Duke Crepsta and his wife looked intrigued. Jax could not deny that the picture he painted embodied the ideals of any benevolent ruler, but she wondered about the truth behind Darian's 'sincere character', as he labeled it. If he was even remotely aware of Lucien's shady dealings, then how could she trust him?

Striking while the coals were still hot, Lucien jumped back in. "The Cetachi Accord declares that Cetachi will be inducted into the Realm of Virtues as a recognized democratic state and be equal in influence to that of a dukedom. I open the floor for discussion." He waved his hand to the center of the table as he sat down next to Landon.

Duke Mensina cleared his throat. "I think there are lingering questions that must be answered first." His gaze rested squarely on Darian. "Master Fangard, why are you so keen to see Cetachi as an elected state, rather than a dukedom?"

Paling slightly as he visibly struggled to find the right words, Darian stood up to address the room once more. "I have the utmost respect for the bloodlines seated at this table, as well as those who were not able to join us in person." He walked slowly around the cluster of chairs, clearly still trying to piece together an adequate answer. "But I can respect people and disagree with their methods at the same time. I was born the son of a baker. In the structure of your duchies, what would have become of me?" He paused, although he had asked a rhetorical question. "I would have become a baker. Instead, I stand before you as an elected official, a leader selected by my peers. Those of us who are common-born yearn for more than just the life we were born into. We yearn for progress and success and the chance to do something more than follow in our parents' footsteps." Darian abruptly turned and locked eyes with Jax. "Duchess Jacqueline, I hear you are very close with your lady's maid and that even though she is more than qualified to be your next lady-in-waiting, you will not bestow the honor on her because she is common-born."

Jax felt as if she had been drenched in a bucket of ice water. Beside her, a soft gasp escaped Perry's lips. How had Darian gotten hold of this sensitive information?

"Why should the origins of her birth matter? Why should that determine her path for the rest of her life? Has she not worked hard and proven her dedication to you?" Darian challenged, his focus solely on Jax. "You see, that is my argument against Cetachi being a dukedom. My people would simply be stuck right where they are. Maybe there would be some greater level of protection, but I would still be a baker's son or some lowly equivalent." Darian's gaze burned with fervor. "A free, elected state will allow for the progress and development that have stunted the duchies for so long."

"And tell me, Darian," Jax answered, summoning a steely exterior, "who will bake the bread in this free state? Who will be the ones to work these lowly equivalent jobs, as you call them? Your words are not only offensive to the people in this room, but to all throughout our prosperous realm. People like your father are the individuals who make our duchies thrive. Woodworkers, tailors, merchants, bakers. These are all admirable roles, supporting the greater good in their honest and noble work. Perhaps in the wilds of Cetachi, a baker is not respected, but in Saphire, a baker is the soul of his village, his family in want of nothing." She stood up, challenging the young man to come closer. "Considering how sheltered Cetachi has been all these years, your people likely do not fully understand how an enterprise like a duchy actually operates. And perhaps it has never been properly explained to you." She risked an accusing look at Lysandeir, whose lips lifted in a snarl. "Our common-born citizens do have the opportunity to achieve wealth and security within our system. You so freely mentioned my maid Uma. Do you think her family is in want of anything? Do you think her mother was also a lady's maid? No, her mother was a skilled nurse and her father was a village physician. Uma's destiny was not laid out before her because her parents were healers. No, she was able to take her own path."

"As a servant?" Darian shot back.

"As a companion to the most influential leader in the Realm of Virtues." Jax's fingers curled with her echoing retort. "So, yes, while a common-born individual in Saphire will not one day wake up ruling the land, it is naive and ignorant to think that our people are oppressed."

Silence blanketed the room as Darian's eyes darted to Maegus and Lucien, a subtle panic beginning to set in on his face.

Jax smoothed her dress as she sat back down. "If you hope to persuade a body of people who have been educated and developed to be leaders since the moment of their birth, I suggest you secure a better defense."

"You think just because you were born into it, that it's your right to rule?" Darian asked with candidness that surprised her. "Just because you had a fancy education, that makes you suitable for the job? What if there was someone in Saphire who could do it better, Your Grace? Would you allow them to sit on the throne? If you think you are the best person for the position, what would you do if there was someone better than you?"

The flurry of questions left her flustered, but before she opened her mouth to respond, Duke Pettraud barked out a laugh. "You think by convincing us that we are unfit to rule our own duchies, you will get our votes, boy? You have a lot to learn."

"I think we should take a preliminary vote to see where things stand," Jaquobie suggested, his eyes sweeping over the room. Tensions were beginning to rise high. "That will allow us all to frame the remainder of the summit's discussions."

"Agreed," Duke Crepsta declared from his perch, holding his wife's hand with white knuckles.

A clearly rattled Lucien ran a hand through his flaming hair. "Very well. All those currently in favor of the Accord, please raise your right hand."

Jax's eyes darted around the room, tallying the votes. Both Duchess Tandora and Lysandeir raised their hands without hesitation. The High Courtier from Zaltor conferred with his other three courtiers before raising his. The High Courtier from Hestes also put a hand in the air. Four votes out of the remaining ten in play. Hope sparkled inside her chest.

"All those against the Accord for statehood." The Duke could have not sounded less thrilled.

Jax's hand went straight up, accompanied by Dukes Mensina, Crepsta, and Pettraud.

The cluster of advisors from Beautraud and Kwatalar exchanged uncertain looks within their groups, but their High Courtiers' hands ultimately remained on their laps.

"A tie," Lucien groaned with dismay, tossing a handkerchief he'd been wiping across his forehead to the table.

"And in the event of a tie, the Accord fails," Jaquobie redundantly informed the group.

Darian nearly leaped out of his chair in undignified anguish. "Well, that was only a cursory vote, right? We still have three days of the summit left to mount our arguments."

He didn't point out the obvious…that thanks to the vote, each side now knew precisely who they needed to persuade. Jax simply had to ensure that either Beautraud or Kwatalar voted their way, and they would be home free. She felt a stab of worry, for she suspected Lucien was already trying to figure out a way to manipulate both duchies to support the Accord.

"May the best man win," Duke Pettraud said with a harsh guffaw, standing in front of his seat. "I think it's best we all break for lunch, don't you, Lucien?"

Perry's father didn't give their host time to object. He was already escorting Duchess Tandora out of the room.

The High Courtiers surveyed their counterparts as the other leaders rose, all except Jax and Perry. It hadn't escaped her notice that many of the attendees had been scribbling notes as they sat around the table all morning. She wanted to take a moment to privately examine the different handwritings to see if any of them matched the note burning a hole in her dress pocket.

Jaquobie was the last to leave, trailing after Lysette, Landon, and Lawrence, all of whom cast lingering, suspicious stares at Jax and Perry as they followed their fuming father to the banquet hall.

"Tough crowd," Perry said with a low whistle.

"We certainly learned quite a lot." Jax bit her lower lip. "The most urgent being we have a spy in our midst."

Perry looked shocked. "What makes you say that?"

"When Darian prattled on about Uma, about me wanting to make her my new lady-in-waiting. She and I discussed that privately during our carriage ride, Perry. Only she and I knew about it." The dread welling in Jax's stomach made any thoughts of hunger disappear.

She watched Perry's cheeks grow pink with unease. "Well, that's not entirely true, Jax. You see...dear Uma came to visit Hendrie yesterday afternoon while you were taking your bath. I overheard them talking about it through the connecting door attached to my suite. She was a bit upset that her lineage was holding her back from being your formal companion. And you know how passionate Hendrie has been on the subject of late. I had to interrupt and smooth things over with both of them about your hands being tied on the matter."

Jax's eyes narrowed into slits, not at all appreciating that Perry had kept her in the dark. "That still doesn't explain how Darian got hold of the information."

"Well, that's not the whole story," Perry continued. "When I went back into my room, I noticed the hallway door was ajar. I thought I had closed it when I left, but as I went to shut it, I saw Jaquobie scurrying away. He very well could have overheard everything from the adjoining room."

"Why on earth would Jaquobie share that information to be used against me?" An annoyed Jax snapped the question, although she knew Perry couldn't be blamed.

Her fiancé shrugged as he reached for a piece of parchment. "You'll have to ask him that."

"Oh, I intend to," she pledged, but put those thoughts aside for the moment. She picked up an ink-covered scroll and held it side-by-side to the note found on Lady Gwen. "This doesn't match."

"Nor do these. No one in the Beautraud or Zaltorian delegations forged George's name."

After shuffling through all the leftover parchment, they were able to determine that no one from Beautraud, Zaltor, Kwatalar, or Mensina had written the deceptive note.

"It doesn't look like my father's writing, so I think we can rule him out as well," Perry said as he took a harder look at the piece of paper.

Disappointed that no one from the remaining duchies had left behind any notes for them to review, Jax tucked the paper back inside her dress pocket. "Speaking of your father, you might want to prepare for your luncheon with him. Didn't Jaquobie say he was expecting you in his chambers at one?"

"I almost pushed the meeting out of my mind." Perry gave her a lame smile.

"You don't have to speak with him if you really don't want to, Perry. I can arrange a meeting with him instead."

"I'll be fine. Virtues, if you and your grandfather made amends, there may be hope for me yet," Perry jested. "Shall I escort you to the banquet hall before I pop over?"

Jax's nose wrinkled. "I can walk a few hundred feet by myself without getting attacked, Perry."

Perry frowned at her attitude. "You know George would have my head if I let you walk alone."

"She doesn't need to walk alone, Lord Pettraud. I can escort the Duchess to lunch." Darian's silky voice floated in from the doorway. He stood there, hands behind his back, watching them with interest.

Jax stiffened. How long had he been watching them?

The Governor stepped forward, inching his way to the center of the room. "I thought I might have misplaced my suit jacket in here this morning. I could have sworn I brought it with me before our peace talks started." He surveyed his abandoned seat. "But I guess not. Shall we go to lunch?" He offered her his extended arm.

Perry's stone-faced expression suggested that he would rather sever his own leg than allow Jax to be alone with this man, but she cut him off with a bright smile. "How kind. Yes, Darian, that would be lovely. I'll see you this afternoon, Lord Pettraud," she chirped, leaving a speechless Perry in her wake as she readily accepted the outstretched hand of her dashing rival.

Chapter Twelve

"I do give you credit for keeping things civilized outside the discussion chambers, Darian," Jax said as they strolled through the stone fortress, making their way to the banquet room for the second time that day.

"I meant what I said about respecting the ducal families, your bloodline in particular. You impressed me in there, Duchess. I was expecting my comments about your servant to throw you off guard."

Darian's transparency made her smile. "Oh, you succeeded, but my years of training to be an unflappable sovereign have at least helped me in that regard." She couldn't help but poke fun at his own words. "But that servant you mentioned so flippantly is my dear friend, so I'd appreciate it if you didn't drag her name through the mud for your own political gains."

"Perhaps I picked the wrong duchy to persecute," Darian admitted with a mischievous grin.

She could tell that her disclosure of genuine friendship with Uma surprised him. "Perhaps you did," she agreed. She voiced her next question with composed bluntness. "Who informed you about Uma's desires to be named my lady-in-waiting?"

His answer came without pause. "A gentleman never reveals his source."

Jax studied his strong profile. He would indeed make for a

handsome figurehead, his good looks no doubt a factor in securing the confidence of his people back home. "I thought we were going to hear more about how you came to be the prodigal son of Cetachi."

A scowl marred Darian's handsome features. "I thought so too, but Lysandeir wanted to jump right into defining the Accord." He looked at his feet as his cheeks flushed. "It was my intention to make the council understand all the pain and anguish that have finally led the Cetachi people to this pivotal moment."

"Well, tell me now," Jax said, stopping in her tracks. She scanned the hall and found a nook by a large window overlooking the white mountaintops. Motioning Darian to claim a seat, she perched on the windowsill and prepared to listen.

He eyed her warily, as if concerned she was setting some kind of trap. "Where should I start?"

"The election. How did it come about?" Jax questioned.

"It's hard to believe it happened over six months ago," he began. "During the spring equinox. We had barely made it through the winter—the southern region I hail from was incredibly short on food. The heads of the civil tribes met out of desperation. We all knew we had to come up with something, or Cetachi would indeed be lost to the wilds. For decades, the region has been sinking deeper and deeper into decay, cut off from the rest of the realm." His eyes took a downward cast as he relayed the painful memory. "So, I convinced my tribal leader to let me speak to the group. I explained my vision that if we could work together to create a stable nation, we could successfully integrate into the realm. The leaders agreed with me, so all that was left to do was pick someone to unite us all."

"And let me guess, you had a solution for that, too?" Jax smiled as she arched an eyebrow.

"It seemed only logical. Why not let a group of people choose who would lead them into a new era?"

"Lucky for you, it seems," Jax said with a wry twist of her lips.

"Several people did come forward, promoting their ability to lead. We had debates and every inch of our lives examined by the people. It's not as if I hoodwinked anyone." He paused as he crossed his arms in defense. "My actions spoke for themselves. I advocated for my people long before Cetachi as a whole decided to do something about it. My dedication and service proved to the electorate that I was ready to lead."

"You mentioned earlier that this all came about from a meeting of the civilized tribes," she said. "Are there others in Cetachi who oppose your plans?"

Darian took a deep breath. "I suppose you would find out sooner or later, Duchess, but yes. There are hosts of wild men roaming the borders who are against changing our ways. They've been more difficult to wrangle these past few months. When I was elected, I ordered all raids to cease under penalty of death."

Jax leaned back, stunned that Darian had the backbone to take such severe measures. "From what I've heard, the raids did eventually cease."

Darian nodded darkly. "But there have been some murmurs of them resurfacing in recent weeks. I had hoped Maegus would be able to put a stop to it while I was here, but—" Darian broke off, as if realizing that he'd revealed his displeasure at the Warden's appearance with one too many people. "The wild men have been assaulting our borders with Pettraud, and even outposts in Lysandeir and Tandora. I thought the resurgence would cause the Duke to pull his support for the Accord, but it seems to have only intensified his desires to see me rightfully seated as head of state so I can put a finite end to the raids."

Jax scoffed. "Don't you find the timing of it all a bit odd? From your tone, it sounds like Pettraud is the one taking the brunt of the raids. Pettraud, which happens to oppose the Accord."

Her opponent's head cocked. "What are you getting at, Duchess?"

Jax clasped her hands in her lap, lacing her fingers together. Looking as pious as she could, she replied, "Considering your claims of a righteous character, I'm interested in what you'll do with this information I'm about to share. You were overheard upon your arrival here saying that you had not seen Duke Lysandeir in months. Yet, I have confirmed reports that he has been traveling to a Cetachi outpost for private meetings on a regular basis."

Darian's mouth nearly plunged to the stone floor as he leaped to his feet. "What? That can't be possible. Where did you hear this?"

"A lady never reveals her sources," Jax mimicked.

Snarling under his breath, he stepped closer to her until he was mere inches away. "How do I know you're not lying to me?"

"Look at the truth in my eyes and tell me if I look like a liar to you, Governor," she snapped. "If you really care about your people, you better reexamine who you are keeping company with." Her amethyst gaze burned with a silent plea for the young man to see reason. "You are not the only person here who wants what's good for the people of this realm."

He took a step back and cleared his throat. "I appreciate the information, Duchess." He turned from her to stare out the frost-laden window. "It seems I can trust no one to help my cause," Darian said, immense sadness sagging from his shoulders.

Jax stood up from her perch, from where she could feel the chill from the wintry winds outside sweeping under the panes. "If your cause truly revolves around pulling Cetachi out of the darkness with a seat at the realm, then let me help you."

Darian raised his chin. "Trade one snake for another? You just want to package Cetachi up into a nice little duchy and continue with the status quo." He raked his hands through his tousled hair, steaming.

"I did when I arrived, I will admit that much. But I see something special in you, Darian. I see why your people voted for you to lead them to something better. I would not want to deprive them of your spirit." Jax's voice oozed with sincerity.

Darian squinted at her, confused and dazed by their conversation. "What are you saying?"

"I'd like to arrange a private meeting with you this evening after dinner to discuss the future of your homeland. No Lucien, no Maegus, just you. My guardsman will meet you at the bottom of the west wing stairs and escort you to my chambers," Jax directed, delighted by the curiosity dancing in those Cetachi eyes.

"Has this all been some well-laid trap?" he asked.

Jax's grin gleamed. "You'll have to spring it to find out."

Chapter Thirteen

Despite their longwinded discussion, Jax reckoned they still had time to sit down for a brief lunch before the afternoon session began. She and Darian meandered to the banquet room in contemplative silence. It was encouraging to know he was open to meeting with her to discuss ways to bring Cetachi the prosperity it so long deserved.

Just as the two reached the archway, she heard a scuffle behind her.

"Jax!" Perry's voice called from the opposite end of the hallway.

The panic in his voice unnerved her. She quickly excused herself from Darian's company and hurried toward Perry's approaching figure.

"Virtues, Perry, what is it?" she asked, breathless.

"I need you to come with me right now." Forgetting proper etiquette, he grabbed her by the arm and rushed her along a corridor that dipped deep into the castle before climbing a steep set of tower stairs.

"Do you even know where you are going?" A cramp poked at Jax's side as they ascended the seemingly endless staircase.

"My father wasn't too pleased about being shunned to the south tower, either," Perry commented wryly, giving her a moment to catch her breath.

"This is where your father is staying?" Jax was stunned. She would have thought the Duke would have been given the courtesy of a suite closer to the action.

"Crepsta and Tandora are in the north wing, and Mensina, Beautraud, and Zaltor are in the east. We seem to be the only ones in the west tower, which my father pointed out to Lysandeir. Apparently, there are a few rooms above us that are currently being renovated and not suitable for guests," Perry summarized.

Jax thought back to the sounds she'd overheard on the floor above while taking her bath. "No wonder your father was so grumpy last night. You'd think Lucien would have made sure the renovations were complete before this summit," she mused. "But why did you drag me all the way out here?"

"My father and I planned to take lunch in his suite. He sent his valet to retrieve a selection of items from the banquet hall. We were starting to wonder where he had gone off to, when we heard a serving tray clatter to the floor out in the hallway." Perry looked as ashen as the snowcapped mountains silhouetted outside. His pace slowed as they approached a looming shadow up ahead.

A groan escaped Jax's lips as comprehension flooded her senses. She knew that look of distress in Perry's eyes. She'd seen it just last night.

As they arrived at the landing, her eyes examined the body that lay on the floor. A river of blood ran dangerously close to the overhang, threatening to drip on unsuspecting passersby below. Briefly closing her eyes to summon her courage, Jax then tiptoed next to the lanky frame of Duke Pettraud's uniformed valet. "Was he like this when you opened the door?"

Perry nodded. "Not thirty seconds passed from the time we heard the racket of the platter to when we opened the door." He shook himself free of the haunting images. "Not a soul was in sight. I looked around for a moment and then went to find you."

Jax glanced over her shoulder at the winding staircase. "No one could have gotten to the bottom in that short amount of time without you seeing them." She examined the landing. The only escape routes were the door to Duke Pettraud's suite and a window. She dashed over to the sill and inspected the ledge. "Snow has been brushed off the window pane, Perry." She motioned for him to join her, pointing to the bare lip of the window outside. "Someone pushed the glass open and climbed out onto the ledge."

"But I would have seen them in the window when I came out here."

In response, Jax pushed the window wide open, wind and snow biting at her exposed skin as she leaned outside. Peering down, trying to ignore the plummeting depths below, she saw a rope dangling from the outside wrought-iron frame. "Looks like our culprit climbed down to a window on the floor below," she guessed with grim satisfaction.

"We're dealing with a madman, Jax," Perry sputtered. "Who would take such a risk, let alone in this weather?"

"Someone who had nothing left to lose, I assume," she muttered before turning her attention back to the dead valet. "Where is your father?"

"I ordered him to stay in his room with a few of his sentries." Perry looked at the closed door. "His Captain of the Guard went to fetch Lysandeir's men."

Taking a moment to get a closer look at the body, Jax's nose wrinkled. "Well, I think Lucien will be hard pressed to cover this up as an accident." She pointed to the sleek dagger that jutted from the man's bloody neck.

Perry looked at the knife, his pale face gaining a green pallor. "There's no ducal signet on the hilt."

"Right." Jax looked at her betrothed with veiled dread. "That means this blade was forged in Cetachi." She moved toward Duke Pettraud's closed door, careful not to step in the spilled food and wine from the discarded serving tray. "I'd like a word with your father before Lysandeir swoops in."

Perry obliged, knocking softly on the door before them. "Father, Duchess Jacqueline needs a word with you."

The door whipped open. "Virtues, you brought the Duchess up here?" Duke Pettraud sputtered as he ushered his son and future daughter-in-law into the foyer of his suite.

"Hardly the first time I've dealt with such a strenuous situation, Duke. Please, before Lucien arrives with his men, have you received any threats since you arrived here?" Jax went straight to the point of her inquiry. The fire in her amethyst eyes compelled the shaken man to speak the truth.

"Threats? No. I mean, Lucien and the Cetachi fellows probably wouldn't have the nicest things to say to me after this morning's session, but no one has approached me directly."

"No letters left for you or your valet?" she pressed.

The Duke threw his arms up in frustration. "Letters? Goodness, girl, what are you going on about? No, I simply sent my man down to fetch Percival and I some lunch and he comes back dead!"

Jax blinked at the rare use of Perry's given name. "Did your valet know anyone at this summit who would want to cause him harm?"

"No!" Pettraud roared, reaching the end of his patience. "Clouse was as innocuous as a shadow. That's what made him such a damn good valet. Virtues, what a shame." The Duke bowed his head as the sorrow hit him. "Who could do this to him?"

Jax glanced at Perry, who looked as helpless as she felt. "I don't know, Your Excellence. First, Lady Gwendolyn is killed, now this…"

The Duke held up a hand. "Lucien told us all Lady Gwendolyn slipped on the stairs. Are you saying someone murdered her, as well?"

Jax pursed her lips together, figuring that with another attack, the inhabitants of the castle needed to know a killer was among them. "I saw telltale bruising around her neck. It looked like she was strangled before being tossed down the stairs."

Pettraud balled his hand into a fist, punching the cushioned backing of the nearest chair. "And Lysandeir has just been letting us roam the castle freely while a lunatic is on the loose?"

"That could be the least of his crimes," Perry mumbled.

Jax cringed at his words.

"What do you mean, boy?" the imposing man barked at his son.

Jax's shoulders sagged in relief as Duke Lysandeir's booming voice interrupted them before Perry could spill too much more crucial information.

"You and a dead body again, Duchess," Lucien sneered with unrelenting malice, his eyes going straight to Jax as he barged into the entryway of Pettraud's suite.

"I think you'll find this time that murder is irrefutable," she said, issuing a challenge for him to otherwise explain the valet's death. She walked back out to the landing, where a group of palace guards combed the gruesome scene, knowing the others would follow. "That blade sticking out of the valet's neck looks to be forged in Cetachi." She sent her glaring wrath the Duke's way.

Lucien waved her comment aside. "Merchants sell Cetachi-made goods all over the realm."

"And royals and High Courtiers are their best buyers?" Jax laughed at the absurdity. "Or are you hiding someone else within your castle walls, Lucien?"

The Duke met her gaze and for the first time, she saw his bravado falter. "Countless servants traveled here with each of the delegations," he pointed out. "Contrary to what you might believe, Jacqueline, the world is much bigger than you and your inner circle. My men will have their work cut out for them questioning everyone."

It pleased Jax that he intended to treat Clouse's death as foul play. "Well, I can vouch for Darian Fangard's whereabouts around the time this happened. He and I took a little stroll together to discuss Cetachi's best interests." She darted a look at Perry.

He nodded that he understood it was time for them to depart.

"Due to this incident, it's probably in good taste not to reconvene the summit until at least tomorrow morning, don't you agree?" Jax said to the Duke with a demure grin. "I imagine you'll need time to find the killer and ensure the safety of your remaining guests." Still smiling, she turned to leave, knowing the enraged Duke would stew over what she had so expertly let slip. On top of Clouse's death, Lucien now had to contend with her undermining his deal with Cetachi.

Without further protest, Jax and Perry dashed down the staircase, eager to leave the ghastly scene behind. But, once they had put a flight of stairs between them and murder, Jax held out her arm to halt Perry in his tracks.

"What now?" he asked with a groan, clearly overwhelmed by the events of his disrupted luncheon.

She pointed to one the doors lining this area of the landing. "If I recall correctly, the window our culprit climbed down into should be in this room," she guessed, twisting open the brass doorknob without a second thought.

Perry watched her wordlessly as she entered the small chamber, which was full of brooms, mops, and buckets. "A closet. Likely always unlocked for the staff." Jax cursed under her breath, knowing anyone could gain access to this. Moving over to the window, she noticed a few broom handles strewn across the floor, left behind in a clutter. "Looks like someone was here recently, and left in a bit of a hurry," she mused. One look through the window confirmed her suspicions. The snow had been disturbed on the window pane, just like the one on the floor above them.

"So, someone kills Clouse, climbs down the window and waits in here until the coast is clear?" Perry said, laying out the puzzling scenario.

As his words took hold in her mind, she stifled a gasp. "Perry! The killer likely waited until you ran down the stairs to get me." She reflexively gathered him close in her trembling arms. "They could have attacked you from behind." Her last words were lost to a silent stream of frightened tears that she'd been steeling away since their encounter with Lady Gwen's body last night.

Perry clutched her against him, the vibrations of his racing heart confirming that he, too, knew how much danger he'd been in. "Well, they didn't, and there's no use fretting about it now." His warm lips pressed against her forehead. "Jax, someone wicked is stalking these halls. I don't encourage putting yourself in harm's way, but if you are going to solve this, I hope you do it quickly."

She pulled back from him, her face firm with resolve. "I can't figure out why someone would target a lady-in-waiting and a valet. I mean, our rivals in Cetachi are all about elevating the common man. Why would they attack the very people they claim to support?"

"Well, Lady Gwen was from a noble house. Perhaps they thought a valet would be, too?" Perry considered. "You said yourself in front of all those people that neither Darian nor Maegus really know or understand life outside of their borders."

"Yes, but still, why do it? How does targeting nobles help their cause in any way?" Jax frowned. "It just goes to prove that Cetachi is a lawless land of rebellion, not fit for statehood. And besides, Darian was with me at the time of the murder."

"Then we need to see what Maegus was up to," Perry said with a grimace.

"Agreed, but let's reconvene with George and my grandfather. I want to fill them both in." Jax shooed Perry out of the broom closet, and together they began retracing their steps back to familiar territory.

"Are you going to involve Jaquobie at all?" Perry asked.

Jax tucked a loose strand of her caramel-colored hair behind her ear. "Not at the moment. I'm still trying to figure out why he would have shared Uma's desire to be my lady-in-waiting with Darian. It makes me sick to think he might be plotting against us."

"What if he didn't tell Darian…" Perry's voice trailed off, and he suddenly ducked behind a column in the west wing hallway, pulling Jax with him.

"What's this abo—?" she sputtered, but he clasped a hand over her mouth.

Pointing down the hall, he whispered in astonishment, "Why, my eyes must be playing tricks."

Jax blinked a few times herself, almost pinching her own arm to reassure her brain that her eyes were not deceiving her. "Is that Jaquobie and…*Lysette*?" she exclaimed in a dumbfounded gasp.

Up ahead of where she and Perry stood, two figures were entwined in the shadows, the tall, sinewy man tenderly stroking the face of the red-haired young woman less than half his age.

Jax looked to Perry in total bewilderment. *What do I do?* she asked her fiancé with her wide eyes.

Perry shrugged in reply, but she saw his muscled chest shaking as he tried to restrain the growing laughter. The scene before her did not stroke her funny bone at all. In fact, the more she watched the blatant flirtation, the angrier she became.

"Jaquobie!" she yelled with boiling authority, watching as the High Courtier jumped out of his skin to scurry away from Lysette's coquettish embrace.

"Duchess, I…" he stammered, his head darting around wildly until he spotted her from her hidden post. "I didn't hear you approach."

At least he has the decency to look guilty, Jax thought with a twinge of satisfaction. She looked from his oily hair and sweaty face to Lysette's flawless, yet blushing expression. "Please excuse us, Lady Lysette."

The princess summoned what dignity she had left and retreated, gathering her skirts as she hurried away.

As soon Lysette was out of sight, Jax couldn't stop herself from thwacking Jaquobie's shoulder. "Have you gone mad?" She yelled with punctuated anger. "Please tell me you have, because there is no other explanation as to why my High Courtier is behaving like a fool!" She edged closer to hysteria with each word.

Jaquobie, in all the years she had known him, had never looked so feeble and flustered as he appeared before her now. "Duchess, I can explain," he finally managed to say.

"Then please do," she said with exaggerated slowness, towering over his hunched figure.

"Not here. Please, let us return to the privacy of our chambers." In his shame, his request was barely audible.

She had to agree with him, for anyone could appear in the hallway at any moment and overhear this debacle. "Move. *Now.*" She ushered him up the west wing stairs with a reprimanding swat.

Perry trailed behind them, still trying to control his laughter.

Chapter Fourteen

Jax forcefully shoved Jaquobie into one of the armchairs in her suite, the chastened man not bothering to protest her lack of manners. "You have five minutes to explain why you've been delivering our secrets to the hands of our enemies, or I will chain you up and lock you away in the dungeons when we return to Saphire." Her gaze exuded venom.

Jaquobie's face dissolved into confusion. "Enemies? What are you talking about, Jacqueline?"

She stared down at him. "*I* am the one asking the questions here, High Courtier." She folded her arms, noticing Perry, Uma, George, and Hendrie all gathering around the edges of the large room. "Have you betrayed us to Lysandeir?"

"No! Of course not, Duchess! I would never..." Jaquobie looked like a caged animal. "I am nothing but loyal to your court. You must know that to be true."

She assessed his pleading gaze and decided no lies simmered beneath it. "Then how did Darian come to learn about Uma's desire to be my lady-in-waiting?"

Shame bloomed in Jaquobie's amber eyes. "Ah," he said, clearing his throat, "yes, I suppose that was my fault. You see..." he trailed off for a moment, collecting his thoughts, "Lysette had asked me what her odds were of being selected for your lady-in-waiting, and I flippantly made the remark that considering only your lady's maid was gunning for the post, her chances were good, since Uma is not of noble blood." Jaquobie's eyes cast downward, the picture of regret. "I was stunned to hear Darian use it against us, but Lysette swears she only told her brothers how much she admires your being so close to your lady's maid."

"And that didn't make you think her brothers were plotting against us?" Jax's mouth dropped at his carelessness.

"At first, perhaps, Your Grace. But Lysette claims her brothers did not share the information with anyone. Remember, the Cetachi delegation are in the same tower as the Lysandeirs. They could have very easily been overheard at any point."

"You believe her?" The question came from George.

Jaquobie answered him, but his eyes never left his Duchess. "Yes. She wouldn't lie to me, nor her brothers to her."

Jax took a moment to carefully examine Jaquobie's earnest expression before presenting her next question. "Why is Lysette so keen to be my lady-in-waiting? She's hardly paid me any attention since our introduction. Have you considered that her motives might not be pure?"

Jaquobie sprang to life at the accusation. "Lysette is innocent in all of this. She was genuinely sorry that Darian found out about Uma. In fact, she was mortified. She was afraid I would call off our—" he faltered for a moment before his shoulders drooped in defeat. "If I am to be accused of anything, Duchess, it's of having selfish motives for her appointment as your lady-in-waiting. You see, I have been courting Lady Lysette since we met at a gala in Hestes this past spring."

Jax's mouth dropped open, and she could hear stifled gasps from her companions behind her. "Courting her?"

"Yes, we met one night after a symposium hosted by a group of Hestian scholars. I was at the capital, negotiating some new trade agreements on your behalf, and I stopped in to listen. She was in the audience, and we struck up a conversation." His cheeks now matched the color of Lysette's fiery hair. "We've been...close ever since."

Jax recalled Lysette's fondness for Hestes and wondered if that was the reason. "If I remember your scheduled travels this past summer, Jaquobie, you went to Hestes quite a bit."

He shrank under her stare. "Yes, Duchess. I may have embellished the necessity of some of my state visits needing to be in person."

"So you have been courting Lysette this entire time, feeding her information to funnel to her father," Jax accused with grim anger.

"No! We never talked about matters of state. Lysette can't stand how it's driven her father to cruelty." Jaquobie sounded as helpless as he looked. "You'll notice how upset she was at your mention of being a reminder of her mother. That's because Lysandeir beats his children!" His face turned to a mask of rage, his eyes burning with vengeful fire. "That's right, the monster beats them because he blames them for his treasured wife's death."

Jax felt her heart break for the triplets, ashamed that she had unknowingly triggered painful memories with her own words. "That's horrific, to blame innocent children."

"That's why Lysette is so desperate to leave. But her father would never allow it unless the price was right. And unfortunately, the promise of an engagement to a foreign High Courtier is not enough." Jaquobie colored once more at his admission of his plans. "That is why I wanted you to offer her the post of lady-in-waiting. Lysandeir couldn't refuse the chance to place his daughter in the confidences of another court."

"So, you wanted me to name Lysette as my most trusted companion, all so that you could marry her once she was out of her father's violent clutches?" Jax could not believe she was asking this of her shrewd and rigid advisor.

"Yes, Duchess. At the Aldereen Inn, I told you I didn't need your assistance finding love, but it turns out I do need your help freeing it." Jaquobie hung his head.

She looked over her shoulder at the faces of her friends. While they indeed all appeared shocked, she couldn't help but notice the trace of pity in their eyes. "Jaquobie, why didn't you just tell me all this was happening?" She knelt, placing her hands over his, which were trembling. "I would have helped you figure out a way to get her out of here that didn't involve sneaking behind my back."

Jaquobie lifted his head, his lips parted in surprise. "You would have done that for me?"

She gave him a chastising look. "I'm offended you have to ask, sir. You've known me since the moment I was born, and you were one of my father's closest friends. Why would I deny you such happiness?" Her heart softened as she saw Jaquobie's eyes fill with bright tears.

"Well, Jax," he whispered, using her nickname for the first time, "I always got the sense that you didn't like me very much. After all, I've been a little bit of a thorn in your side."

"A little thorn?" Jax chuckled. "While we may have our differences, you are a loyal and faithful advisor to my duchy. You are someone I trust, and while we may not be fast friends," she paused, eying the crinkle in the man's eyes, "I still do wish for you to find happiness. Maybe it will finally melt that icy exterior of yours." She stood up with a satisfied smile. "I will arrange for Lysette to return with us."

"As your lady-in-waiting?" Jaquobie asked, eyes filled with hope.

"I'll do what is necessary," Jax replied, her face neutral as she made the promise. "Now that we've got all that out in the open, I think it's time Perry and I bring everyone up to speed on the latest events to befall our little peace summit."

After George placed a few of his guardsmen out in the hall to patrol for any eavesdroppers, Jax recounted the attack on Clouse and Lysandeir's subsequent appearance. She also explained to Uma, Hendrie, and Jaquobie the growing suspicions she had about Lucien's true intentions regarding the Cetachi Accord, and concluded with divulging her plan to offer Darian the opportunity to rule a dukedom.

"So, you have been keeping secrets of your own," Jaquobie said, his slight frown expressing how little he appreciated being left in the dark about the plans Jax and her grandfather had crafted.

Perry, too, looked aghast as she explained her proposal. "That's why you asked me about my brothers? You were going to have Annette marry one of them?"

Jax waved all their concerns aside. "Yes, but those plans have fallen by the wayside now. Darian will be arriving here after dinner for a private meeting. I will send for Duke Mensina and Annette. I want them to be present as well when I outline the full proposition."

"Do you think he'll go for it?" Perry asked, his expression dubious.

George asked the more immediate question. "What if Darian is the one responsible for the killings?"

"I was speaking with him when Clouse was attacked," Jax said with confidence.

"What if he has someone else doing his dirty work?" Hendrie asked. "That Warden of his is a rough-looking fellow. I ran into him earlier. He almost trampled me as we rounded a corner at the same time. Hardly said a word."

"What time was this, Hendrie?" Jax leaned forward eagerly. "Where were you when this happened?"

Hendrie scratched his straw yellow hair as he tried to remember. "I was coming back from the staff lunch. Lysandeir hosted it as a thank you to all the staff supporting the summit. We were in a chamber near the kitchens, not a part of the castle I was very familiar with. We collided as I was leaving."

Jax's gaze slid to Uma's. "Did you attend this as well?"

Uma shook her head. "I stayed behind to keep an eye on things here." Looking sheepish, she explained, "George asked us both to make sure our suites were never left completely unattended."

"What? Goodness, that's what our guards are for!" Jax reprimanded George with a severe look.

"I wanted eyes on the inside as well, Duchess," George said, respectfully but not cowering to her protests.

"I was bringing Uma back a small platter when Maegus ran into me," Hendrie said. "Left me to clean everything up without so much as a glance backward." He grunted. "For all Cetachi's speeches about respecting the common people, he doesn't do a very good job of it."

"Did you notice anything odd about him, other than his lack-of-manners?" Jax asked.

Hendrie closed his chocolate eyes in concentration. "Well, I found it a bit strange that the floor was wet when I was cleaning up the food. Nothing I had on the platter warranted that."

Jax met Perry's eyes. "Perhaps it was melted snow." If Maegus had been the one scaling the southern tower, the raging storm outside would have left its mark.

Hendrie shrugged. "I suppose it could have been. Ruined Uma's lunch, for sure."

"Where did this happen?" George questioned.

"As I said, the luncheon was laid out in a chamber outside the kitchens, which are in the lower floors of the palace, right under the center tower," Hendrie explained.

"Lysandeir's rooms are on the top floor of the center tower," Jaquobie informed them. "I've been there a few times myself to visit Lysette." He met Jax's gaze. "The Cetachi delegation is staying in one of the suites in the lower part of the tower."

Jax's brows lifted. "So, Maegus could have been returning from Pettraud's suite to his own rooms when he ran into Hendrie." She took a moment to consider their next action. "We need to find out if anyone can account for his whereabouts before we confront him. If he's killed two people already, we need to be cautious about provoking him."

"But why would he kill a Pettraudian valet and a Tandorian lady?" Perry asked. "We still haven't figured out his motive."

"Well, like Hendrie mentioned, maybe he doesn't truly embody the morals of this new and free Cetachi." Jax paced the length of the room, her mind frantically at work.

A knock on the door interrupted their session, everyone tensing with slight trepidation.

One of George's men poked his head in, summoning his captain. "Sir, Duke Lysandeir requests an audience with the Duchess."

George shot a look at Jax, silently asking her opinion.

"Show him in," Jax told the guard, her face a blank mask.

Nodding, the guard pushed the door open, revealing a chastened-looking Duke Lysandeir standing in the hall. Pale and withdrawn, he stalked into the room warily, well aware his presence was not wanted.

"May I help you, Lucien?" Jax asked, coaxing the Duke to speak.

"I thought you might want to see this," he said, trembling as he extended his arm.

Jax's eyes dropped to his shaking hand. A piece of parchment fluttered between his fingers. "Where did you find that?"

"It was tucked inside the Pettraudian valet's jacket," Lucien replied. "I believe it is a warning meant for the Duke."

Jax took the note and unfolded it, her eyes scanning the scrawling script.

Reconsider speaking so strongly against the Accord, or this dagger may find your neck next.

She shivered, then read the note aloud to her friends.

Perry came to her side to examine the paper, worry for his father written all over his face. "Someone is threatening him to change his vote."

Jax looked at the script again, something stroking the back of her mind. "Perry, do you recognize this writing at all? I swear it looks like something I've seen before."

Perry narrowed his eyes while concentrating on the parchment. "Hmm. It doesn't look like any of the handwriting from the summit notes I looked at."

"Well, one thing for sure, it's not the same as the writing on the note Lady Gwen had in her hand," Jax concluded. "Which means, we're dealing with more than one threat."

"But this note is clearly telling my father to vote for Cetachi's statehood. The note on Gwen issued no such warning." Perry pointed out.

Lucien spoke up. "Delphinia is already committed to the Accord. Why would she need to be threatened?"

Jax realized that he had no prior knowledge of the note left on Lady Gwen's body before hearing it just now. "I think I'd like to ask her in person," she said decisively, tucking the parchment in her pocket with its predecessor. "George, Perry, come with me. Lucien, I think you and Jaquobie should make an announcement that a man has been killed and that we all need to be alert." Her expression demanded honesty from their host.

Duke Lysandeir nodded in resigned acquiescence. "I'll ask everyone to remain in their suites and station guards outside every door until we know more."

"Thank you," she said, bowing her head ever so slightly. "Send Courtier Roust to meet us at Duchess Tandora's chambers, as well."

With Perry and George trailing behind her, Jax led the way to the north tower. Fifteen minutes later, after getting lost one or two times down the winding hallways, she knocked furiously on the Duchess's door, storming inside the moment it opened.

"Jacqueline? What are you doing here? If you think I'm going to change my vote, you can think again!" Delphinia snapped.

"I'm not here about the Accord, Duchess. I'm here about your lady-in-waiting. Or have you already cleansed her from your mind?" Jax whirled on the old woman, who sank into a chair.

"Of course I haven't. I can't get the poor girl's death out of my head," the Duchess cried, her milky purple eyes tearing up.

Jax was shocked at the surge of emotion exuding from the woman. "You didn't seem too torn up about it earlier."

Delphinia dropped her head into her hands. "That's because I was trying to come to terms with my guilt, you silly girl."

"Guilt?" Jax's ears perked up, shooting looks at an intrigued Perry and George.

"Yes, guilt! It was my fault she was out roaming the halls in the first place." Delphinia stifled a sob. "I saw how desperately she was flirting with your Captain there," she said, motioning to George's trim figure. "I thought I'd play a little joke on the both of them, writing a note asking her to show up at his room." She cast an apologetic look at Captain Solomon's drained face. "I may be old, but I still like to cause a bit of trouble now and then. Only," she said, choking back a sob, "the poor girl died!"

Jax stood there, processing the Duchess's confession. No one else outside her inner circle knew about the existence of the note. If she was to be believed, then Gwen hadn't been lured away to be killed. Had the lady-in-waiting simply been a random victim? It would explain why there was no threat issued to Tandora to change its vote.

Jax wandered around the room, taking stock of a pile of papers bearing the Duchess's seal. She examined the royal signature on the top page. It did not match the writing of either note in her hand. "Duchess, forgive me for nosing into your affairs, but your story does not add up entirely. I have the note you spoke of, but it does not match your hand," she said, pointing to the pile of documents.

Delphinia bristled. "I find it hard to believe you don't have someone sign your official correspondence on your behalf, Jacqueline. Why, I haven't signed my name in years. What you see here is Gwen's work. I hardly ever write anything down, which is why she didn't recognize the note as being written by my own hand." Sniffling, she wiped her reddened nose.

Jax nodded her head with graceful consent. "Thank you for your time, Duchess," she said before abruptly taking leave, Perry and George hurrying after her. She was greeted by Courtier Roust in the hall.

"Thank you for coming, Roust. It's good to still see you alive," Jax said sardonically.

"I'm glad to be here as well. I just heard about Pettraud's valet. Tragic news," Roust sputtered, winded from his journey to the north tower. "This summit has been plunged into darkness. The Duke is locking everyone in their rooms for the night."

"It's good to know he's taking such precautions." Jax breathed a sigh of relief that Lucien was complying with at least some of her suggestions.

Perry arrived at her side, bemused by the quick exit from Tandora's suite. "That's it? That's all you wanted to ask her?" He looked at her like she'd lost her mind.

"There's nothing more she can tell us. Clearly, she hasn't been threatened to change her vote, and she's already on Cetachi's side. I learned what I needed to know," Jax succinctly summarized, her eyes sending him a silent request to trust her. "But I still don't know why Lady Gwen was targeted."

"What do we do in the meantime?" George inquired.

"What I want is for Lucien to place Maegus under guard," Jax wished aloud. "But let's go back to the throne room to see if we can find whose handwriting this is on the second note. I know I've seen it before."

George began to lead the way down to the throne room. "Do we have enough evidence to warrant Maegus's arrest?"

Jax shook her head. "No, it's all circumstantial at best." She sighed. "The dagger could belong to anyone, and a wet floor is hardly incriminating when you realize that this entire palace is encased in snow."

"There's still the possibility that Lucien and Maegus are working together," Perry said. "Just because he brought us the note doesn't mean he's not free of suspicion himself."

"True," Jax conceded. "He might be helping us in order to throw us off his own trail."

After arriving at the abandoned throne room, leaving Roust outside the door to watch, the trio began shuffling through the discarded paperwork once more.

"I don't see anything that resembles the writing on the note." Jax threw her hand out, knocking over the stack of parchment she had just finished searching in frustration. "I could have sworn it looked familiar."

Perry tossed his stack aside in defeat. "We're running out of theories here. I hate feeling like a sitting duck while our killer could be getting ready to make his next move."

Jax looked at her friends with bitter resolve. "We should go speak to Maegus. Confronting him, even without all the facts, may be the only way to put an end to this madness."

Judging from the expression on his face, George knew better than to protest. "I want to go get some of my men to accompany us. Even with the two of us protecting you, Duchess, I wouldn't feel you were entirely safe in the man's presence."

She agreed to his terms, knowing that as sovereign, it would not be wise for her to be so close to possible danger without more protection. "Fine. Let's go back to the tower and get them."

The castle corridors were filled with a ghostly silence as they made their way back to the west wing. They passed a sentry every hundred feet or so, but the absence of chatter and gossip chilled Jax to the bone. The hush was broken up by the sound of swishing skirts ahead. As Jax's gaze settled to the bottom of the tower stairs, she paled. Seeing the woman's regal poise and light hair, it took her a moment to realize that an apparition of Lady Gwen did not stand before her.

"Annette? What are you doing here?" Jax asked, more worried than curious. Lucien had promised the guests would remain in their rooms, protected.

Annette rushed forward, enveloping her niece in a tight squeeze.

"I came to find you, Jacqueline. Father is in an uproar about being barricaded in his room. He caused a scene while I slipped out past the palace guards to find out if you know what's going on."

Jax stiffened in her aunt's arms, her mind exploding into focus. "Oh my goodness," she whispered, pulling away to look Annette directly in the face. "It was you they were after!" She stifled a cry of shock as she realized her aunt had been the intended victim of the first attack.

Looking at a wide-eyed George and Perry, Jax gulped. "That's why we couldn't figure out a motive for Lady Gwen's death. She wasn't meant to die. Annette was," she explained, meeting her aunt's shocked gaze. "Annette's death would have been accompanied by a message threatening Grand-Père to comply with the Accord."

"But when the culprit realized they'd killed the wrong woman…" Perry started.

"They fled the scene without a trace," Jax finished. "That's why Lucien was so keen to label it as an accident. He didn't want anyone digging deeper to uncover the truth behind Gwen's demise."

"So, you think he's really the one responsible?" George's brow furrowed into a hard line.

"It's all beginning to make sense." Jax glanced at Roust, who nodded eagerly for her to continue unraveling the deadly events. "Lysandeir would have known ahead of the preliminary vote that Grand-Père would side with me, which is why the attack intended for Annette came the night before." She continued putting the pieces of the mystery together for her companions. "Once he was able to confirm that both Pettraud and Crepsta would also vote against the Accord, he put the pieces in motion to ensure that wouldn't happen." She reached for George's arm. "You must immediately send some of your men to Crepsta's suite to watch over him and ensure his wife's safety. With Pettraud already warned, he might be next on the list."

George nodded. "Right away. But what are you going to do, Jax?" he asked in return.

"I'm going to collect Jaquobie and my grandfather, then have a word with Lucien to get to the bottom of this," she replied with fierce determination.

"I'll bring Jaquobie back down with me, and then we'll go get your grandfather," George said. "Do not move from this spot, any of you." He glared at Jax, Annette, Roust, and Perry until they all nodded in promise.

"Virtues, what a nightmare," Annette whimpered as George disappeared up the staircase. "That poor woman was killed because she was mistaken for me." A lone tear slinked down her pale cheek.

Jax squeezed her hand, trying to comfort the shaken woman. "I know it's a lot to process, but I can't help but be grateful it was her and not you, as awful as that sounds."

Roust wrung his hands. "If only I'd voiced my misgivings about the Duke's intentions upon your arrival, I could have prevented all this."

Jax laid a palm on the man's shoulder, knowing there were no words she could say that would truly comfort him.

"Do you think my father is all right on his own?" Perry looked at her with concern in his eyes.

"His vote is needed for the Accord. I don't think whoever is behind this would look to eliminate him just yet." Jax could only pray she spoke the truth.

Chapter Fifteen

After a few minutes of tense silence, footsteps were heard clattering down the west wing stairs. Captain Solomon arrived with ten of his men, each gripping the hilts of their swords in readiness. As Jax filled Jaquobie in on the latest developments, George dispatched five of the soldiers to find and secure Duke Crepsta.

"The rest of you," he said with bleak resolve, "follow me."

The tense group arrived at Duke Mensina's doorstep in the eastern tower several minutes later.

"What's going on, Jacqueline? Are you planning a coup or something?" he asked, baffled by the Saphirian guards escorting his daughter and granddaughter.

"I'll explain on the way, Grand-Père. Right now, we must hurry." Jax pulled him out of his suite, paying no attention to his fussy protests.

Jaquobie took the lead from there, having visited Lysette in the central tower where the Lysandeir family resided. It surprised Jax that the sentries did nothing to stop them as the formidable delegation made its way up the winding stairs to the upper levels, arriving at the landing just outside Lucien's study.

Taking a deep breath, Jax rapped on the door, her stomach seizing as she heard shuffling on the other side of the thick wood. "Lucien, open up. We know you're in there!" she yelled, slamming her fist into the door with greater force.

A minute passed before the door inched open a sliver, red hair visible through the crack. "What is the meaning of this?"

George pushed into the room, the Duke stumbling back as the door gave way. "How dare you disturb me in such a manner in my own home!" Lucien roared, his wild eyes darting around the chamber. "I'll have my guards lock you up for this!"

"I think your guards might feel differently about following your orders once they hear you've turned your back on the Virtues, Lucien," Jax challenged as she waltzed into the room with assumed authority. "I doubt they'll be too thrilled to learn their Duke has been ordering the deaths of innocent people and beating his allegedly beloved children."

Lucien's eyes fell on Jax, his face crumpling. "I swear, I never planned for those deaths to happen." His whispered words reached her keen ears alone.

"I find it hard to believe anything transpires in this castle without you knowing it, Duke." She scoffed at his lame attempt to deflect the truth. "You've been trying to undermine this summit from the very start by colluding with Maegus Welles," she accused.

"Where is this outrageous claim coming from?" Lucien roared.

Roust stepped forward. "Those of us in the palace can attest to your regular visits to Cetachi, sir."

"That means nothing!" The Duke's face had turned as red as his hair.

"Then explain what it does mean," a smooth voice demanded from the doorway.

Jax whirled to see Darian leaning against the frame, his brown eyes a well of dark rage. He strode into the room, his gaze never breaking from the Duke's paling face.

"Tell me why you have been visiting my nation in the shadows!" the Governor thundered, betrayal steaming from his pores.

Lucien collapsed in the chair at his desk, his head falling into his hands. "Everything fell apart the moment this whole summit started," he bellowed, shocking the room into silence with his confession. "I was just planning to secure the votes of Beautraud, Zaltor, and Crepsta with some trade agreements, like we did with

Tandora. That's all."

"And you were planning to do this all by yourself?" Jax queried the same time Darian asked, "What trade agreements?"

Jax turned to the Cetachi statesman. "You weren't aware that Lucien gave Delphinia access to harvest the Cetachi forests on her border in exchange for her vote?"

His eyes doubled in size as he turned once more to Lysandeir. "You told me the old woman believed in my cause!"

At that, the corrupted Duke bit out a laugh. "You think a Duchess who has reigned for as long as she has would agree with your pathetic vision? Virtues, you're even more clueless than I thought."

George and Perry each seized one of Darian's arms as he lunged for the Duke.

"Darian, stand down," Jax ordered. She met Lucien's calculated stare. "Maegus is the one arranging those deals on the Cetachi side, isn't he? He forged Darian's name on the agreement you sent to Delphinia." She recalled the stack of papers in the Duchess's chamber.

"I would hardly call Maegus a representative of Cetachi," Lucien revealed with a wicked grin. "He was born in Lysandeir. Did your little investigation uncover that, Duchess? He was the son of one of my most brilliant political advisors. We sent him off fifteen or so years ago to gather information about the wilds of Cetachi. He came back after only three the leader of an entire region. He's been feeding me information for over a decade, helping me plan the right time to march my forces out of these horrible lands and seize Cetachi for myself." Lucien stood up from his desk, his face having transformed into a mask of composure. "We were waiting for just the right opportunity to avoid the wrath of the realm. Then we heard about a little inspirational speech a lowly baker's son gave and we knew our patience was about to be rewarded."

His diabolical smile froze Jax to the bone. "I sent Maegus to befriend this new political hero and plant the seeds of statehood in his young, idealistic mind. All I had to do was play the role of the generous benefactor and the pieces would fall into place." He stalked closer to her, causing half a dozen hands to fly to the hilts of swords. He didn't even bother stepping back. "Cetachi would be declared a state and Darian would assume his position as Governor. Then," Lucien turned his attention to the restrained young man, "an accident would befall him and Maegus, ever the devoted Warden, would assume the position in his stead. For the betterment of the people, he would turn the region over to me, and I would claim it as an expansion of my own duchy." Madness simmered in the Duke's eyes.

"Then why did you deviate from the plan?" Jax asked, keeping her tone even.

"I didn't! I kept my end of the deal. I got Tandora and Hestes on board right away, and secured Zaltor's vote by taking their Ancient Faith leftovers. After Beautraud and Kwatalar abstained in the preliminary vote, I knew I could find something to offer them that would make it worth their while." Lucien's eyes hardened on hers. "I knew there was no sense touching your prestigious group of allies, Duchess. You all were too set in your ways to fall victim to Darian's charms."

Despite his wild expression, Jax felt he was telling the truth. "So, what happened? Why has someone been attacking my allies?"

Lucien slammed his fist onto the desk, the quills and papers rattling under the pressure. "I don't know! At first, I did think the lady's death was an accident, but my physician warned me the markings around her neck were suspicious. I thought someone was trying to sabotage the summit from the other side of the aisle."

Jax remembered how he'd accused her of arranging the woman's death. "What made you change your mind?"

"That note on the body of Pettraud's valet. It reminded me of something Maegus said. When I saw that message, I began to think he had taken measures into his own hands, that he was the reason for this unnecessary bloodshed. For the past few weeks, during our secret meetings, he's been rambling about threatening your allies, Jacqueline, about how it would make our Accord have a stronger chance at passing if your allies were taken out, one by one." He looked out the window at the blinding white snow. "And then you went and rattled him with your words this morning. You pushed him over the edge. *You* pushed him to do this."

"Blame me all you want, Lucien," Jax retorted, "but Lady Gwen was dead long before I spoke out against the Accord. No, *you're* the one who has been working with a killer from the start. I didn't drive anyone to this madness." She steeled herself for more harsh accusations, but Duke Lysandeir remained silent.

He hung his head, shaking it with immense grief. "I just don't understand why he would do this." His voice cracked on the last two words. "We've been planning this for months. We were so close to having the Accord signed without any bloodshed."

"I think it's time to pay my Warden a visit," Darian growled, finally yanking himself free from the steely grips of Perry and George.

Jax motioned for George and Roust to lead the way, feeling drained and devastated by what she had learned. This historic peace summit had never been more than a vile ruse. She couldn't imagine how Darian must hate them all right now. She hated herself for the part she had played in the charade.

After racing down a flight of stairs, they arrived outside the door to Maegus's chambers. Jax gripped Perry's hand for reassurance, as two of her guards dragged Lucien along behind them, keeping a close eye on the disgraced Duke.

Darian took it upon himself to knock, having assumed he'd be the least likely to spook Maegus by paying the man a visit. "Maegus, I need to speak with you." It appeared a struggle for the betrayed man to keep his voice neutral and even.

He received no answer.

Darian cast a strange look Jax's way before knocking again. "Maegus, open up immediately."

Still, they heard no sound or movement on the other side of the stone walls.

"Break down the door," Jax commanded without hesitation, looking to George and few of his men.

With four mighty kicks, the wood splintered open and they all poured into the room.

The sitting area was empty, with no sign that anyone had been using it for at least a few hours. The embers in the fireplace held no warmth as Jax hovered her hand above them, testing their temperature.

The accompanying guards spread out across the

accommodations, but Jax broke away from the others and pushed open the bedroom door.

Sprawled across the four-poster bed was Maegus, blood pooling under his exposed throat.

Shock briefly assaulted her senses, but Jax fought against it and rushed to the man's side. She heard gasps behind her as she touched his frigid skin. "He's been dead for a few hours, if I had to guess." She noticed a splash of dried blood on his right hand. "Darian, do you recall if your Warden was left- or right-handed?"

He answered her from the doorway, his voice heavy with grief as he took in the body of his former friend. "Right-handed, Your Grace."

Jax looked at George and Perry as they drew closer to the body. "I think we can assume that the stain on his hand is Clouse's blood. He was killed before he even had time to properly wash up." Her keen eyes detected bits of food on his jacket. Must be left over from his run-in with Hendrie, she mused to herself.

"Then who killed him?" Perry said, asking the obvious question on everyone's mind.

"It seems every time we think we've gotten the final piece of the puzzle, another gap opens up," George muttered under his breath, clearly unsatisfied with the quick death Maegus received.

Jax backed away from the dead man's side and strode back into the sitting room, where Lucien sat under guard. "I don't think we've ever had all the pieces, have we, Duke?"

The bravado he'd demonstrated in his study had abandoned him, for he sat shuddering under her stare.

"I've been wondering this since my grandfather mentioned it," she declared with a calculated look, "but why did you ride out to meet Maegus in person and escort him to the summit?"

Everyone in their party gathered around the sitting room, waiting for his answer.

"He needed my men to help transport something here," the Duke finally mumbled. "He said it would be useful to our cause."

Jax pushed for the truth. "Do you know what it was?"

Lucien's red mane shook. "No. From the way he presented it to me, I thought it better if I didn't know. It came in a large crate. Maegus asked me to keep it somewhere safe where no one would go.

I had my men put it up at the top of the west wing tower and told everyone else it was under renovation."

Jax's memory flashed back to the noises she heard coming from above her bathtub yesterday afternoon. Had the Duke's men been securing the parcel? Wouldn't they have done that immediately upon their arrival back at the castle earlier that morning?

"Was it some type of weapon you were going to use to intimidate us?" Duke Mensina pressed, his arm hugging Annette close.

Lucien's mouth bobbed open like a fish. "I told you, I don't know what was inside it. I figured it was better for me if I didn't ask too many questions."

"Take us to where your men stored the crate," Jax ordered.

Duke Lysandeir hung his head dejectedly, but nodded.

"Captain Solomon, have some of your men escort my grandfather and aunt back to their quarters," Jax requested. To her family members she said, "I'll come get you when this whole mess is sorted out, but right now I can't be worrying about your safety."

Duke Mensina looked as though he might protest, but Annette silenced him. "Of course, Jacqueline. Be careful," she said as she followed one of the Saphirian guards out of the crowded room.

Jax ousted two more members of their party. "Jaquobie, I want you and Roust to go back to my chambers and check in on Uma and Hendrie." She did not want George and his men to be spread too thin protecting the large group, considering they had no idea what they were up against.

"I know it is useless to suggest, but you should come with us, too, Duchess," Jaquobie said, giving her a lecturing stare.

She didn't even deem it worth a response. "Darian, you should return to your rooms, as well. Obviously, Maegus was not the friend you thought him to be. Who knows what could be waiting up in that tower?"

"If you think I'm going to stay in my room and wait to hear about the other ways I've been stabbed in the back, you're sorely mistaken." Darian fumed with anger as he reached her side.

She knew it would be cruel to command him to stay behind when he had so much at stake. "Very well," she said with a sigh, her attention directed elsewhere. "Lead the way, Lucien."

Duke Lysandeir did not move fast enough for Jax's liking as the remaining group climbed the steps to the top of west tower. Jaquobie and Roust ducked in to the Saphirian apartments as Jax, Perry, George, Darian, Lucien, and a handful of guards disappeared up the remainder of the dark stairs.

Considering no one resided in this portion of the tower, the palace staff had not lit the torches lining the stairwell. George grabbed the last burning flame hanging from the wall, the lone light illuminating the eerie passage.

"Do you hear something?" Perry whispered to Jax, gripping her arm tightly.

She strained to listen past the sounds radiating from their party, but couldn't hear anything of note. "No. Why, do you?"

"I could have sworn I heard laughing."

His words sent ice through her veins.

Shaking away the chill, Jax looked over at a sullen Darian. "You're the one who knew Maegus best. What could he have smuggled into the castle that would be of any use?" She watched the sorrow deepen across his face.

"I *thought* I knew him." His voice was sad and distant, the emotional burden of it all hitting him hard. "I have no more idea than you at this moment, Duchess."

"This is the place." Lucien's voice cracked through the wavering darkness. "We put the crate in here."

Jax and Perry leaned into one another more fiercely, eyes wide as George bent to press the brass handle. To their surprise, the door clicked open to reveal the inside of a sparsely decorated room, likely meant for an accompanying servant if the upstairs had been in use by a royal guest. From the dying sunlight streaming in through the window, Jax could make out a small bed against the far wall and a chair situated next to a fireplace…a *smoking* fireplace.

"Someone just doused the fire," she said with a gasp. Her gaze landed on the center of the room, taking in a massive wooden crate, big enough to sneak a person into the citadel. "Someone's been living here."

"Brilliant observation, Jax."

Jax felt the floor rip out from under her as she recognized that taunting voice. The voice behind the handwriting on that threatening note, that looked so familiar to her, yet she couldn't quite place it.

A figure emerged from the shadows of the far corner, the last of the dying sun searing across her malicious amber eyes.

Aranelda.

Chapter Sixteen

Air refused to fill her lungs as Jax struggled to comprehend what she was seeing. "How?" she finally managed to say. "You died. My men placed your body at my feet."

Arnie sauntered forward, her delight in Jax's confusion written all over her scarred and battered face. "You know, I'm a bit surprised you thought a little bash in the head would do me in. Your men saw me sink to the bottom of Lake Saltrine, yes. I knew they would believe I was dead and return to the palace, but I never thought you'd fall for it too." She laughed with maniacal glee.

"I saw your body," Jax said, her words a mere whimper to those gathered behind her.

Her former lady-in-waiting's sinister eyes narrowed. "Did you forget the secrets we discovered during our summers at the lake?"

Jax felt like her head might burst as she frantically searched her memories, returning to those summers they spent as children exploring the waters. They'd swam through every inch of the Saltrine, discovering its mysteries. "The smugglers' caves."

"There's our clever Duchess." Arnie's grin oozed with satisfaction. "Yes, I swam and hid myself in one of the underwater caves, nearly freezing to death, mind you, but I managed to keep myself alive. Once your men returned to the palace, I found the stash of traveling clothes and supplies dear sweet Marquis had laid out for us during one of his visits home to his charming little family. It still makes me giggle, thinking how he thought I loved him. Men really are hopeless without a woman to guide them, aren't they?" She tittered like a young, innocent girl.

"I saw your body!" Jax roared, coming to life in her fury. "I sent your remains to your family!"

Arnie waved a flippant hand, twirling her long, chestnut hair. "You saw *a* body. The Virtues must have been smiling down on me," she said with a giggle. "In a most fortunate turn of events for me, as I was leaving I happened to run into a young woman traipsing along the riverbed. *Un*fortunately for her, I decided spur-of-the-moment that she'd make the perfect decoy." She shrugged, throwing back a causal glance. "So, I bashed in her face and dressed her in my old clothes. I tossed her in the water to cover my tracks, should your men return to search for a body. I'm surprised you didn't think to give her a closer look." Arnie crossed her arms with a pout on her lips. "I'm actually offended you thought it was me. I have much better bone structure."

Jax flinched at the insanity dancing behind Arnie's wild eyes. "How do you live with the blood on your hands?"

The murderess examined her fingernails, a bored expression settling across her mangled face. "I manage."

"So, what? You escaped Saphire and magically struck up a plan with Maegus?" Jax spat out, unable to fathom the deception of her once-beloved friend.

Arnie sneered. "Maegus. What a pathetic excuse for a man. Absolutely no ambition, even with our friend the Duke here practically handing him his own country." She appraised Lucien with a frown. "Yes, lucky for him, I stumbled right into his secretive little camp just as I was crossing over the Cetachi border. My plan was to lie low once I fled the civilized duchies, to live simple and free for the rest of my days. But," her feline gaze slid back to Jax, "you know me. I enjoy playing the game."

The words stung Jax, causing her to recoil from her former lady-in-waiting.

"You see," Arnie continued, "it was I who dangled a new plan in front of Maegus's greedy hands. Instead of kindly turning over

Cetachi to Lysandeir once all was said and done with their little scheme, I convinced Maegus that we should take Lysandeir for ourselves, establishing the largest and most fearsome duchy in the realm."

"Why did you have to kill those poor people, Arnie?" Jax's eyes filled with tears as she saw the true madness of her former friend.

"Ah, yes, Maegus had a harder time accepting that portion of the plan. But on a stroll through the palace, I was finally able to convince him what needed to be done in order for the summit to swing in our favor."

The whispering threats Roust overheard in the north tower must have belonged to Arnie convincing Maegus of the need for bloodshed, Jax guessed. Her flesh rippled as she pictured Arnie roaming the halls, unleashed upon the world.

Arnie continued her vengeful rant. "Believe me, I did not relish watching someone else do my dirty work for me." She stood mere inches away from Jax, her scarred face fully revealed by the torchlight radiating from George's fist. "Their deaths are on your hands, Duchess. I wanted to strip you of all your dear friends and allies so that you would be left totally alone. So you would know what it felt like for me when you deserted me in that dungeon."

"You killed my parents," Jax whispered through a steady stream of angry tears. "You deserved to be locked away for the rest of your life."

"Well, I think *you* deserved to watch as your allies cowered behind Lysandeir, in fear of death should they associate with you. I wanted you to feel utterly abandoned, because killing off your mother and father didn't seem to do the trick." The crazed look in Arnie's eyes exposed her unhinged mind.

Perry stepped forward, reaching for her arm to pull her back. "Jax, you cannot reason with a madwoman."

She shook away his hand and stayed right where she was. "But things did not go according to plan, did they, Peach?" she said, taunting Arnie with the use of her old pet name.

That haunting amber gaze darkened. "No, the stupid fool killed the wrong woman. After he told me, I knew he couldn't be trusted to see this through. His death sentence was sealed right then and there.

So, after he managed to off the Pettraudian valet and leave my little note for the Duke, I killed him," she stated without a trace of remorse. "I was planning to pay Duke Lysandeir a visit after dinner and ensure he knew to whom he owed his true allegiance."

"I never would have sided with the likes of you," Lucien spat with renewed vehemence. "You ruined everything by poisoning Maegus into being your executioner, just so you could take petty revenge."

Darian stepped from the shadows. "You both failed, because I will do everything in my power to keep Cetachi free from your toxic clutches." He paused, feeling the weight of his words. "Even if it means allowing it to become the thirteenth dukedom in the Realm of Virtues."

Jax felt an inappropriate flash of triumph at his declaration, but knew this was not the time to discuss the region's future.

Arnie, however, saw matters differently. "Not when I've come this far to take it for myself." Faster than anyone else around her could react, she made a desperate lunge for Darian, a dagger glistening in her hand.

Perry yanked Jax out of the way, while George and his men rushed forward. But it was Lucien who catapulted his body, putting himself between Darian and the whirling blade. It landed with a sickening thud, burying itself deep in his fleshy stomach.

Jax watched in horror as blood erupted across the man's tunic. He took a few staggering steps before falling to his knees, his purple eyes glazing over.

"No! You fool! You've ruined everything!" Arnie's carnal screech ripped through to Jax's very core. It sounded like the woman was being burned alive as she screamed and scratched at her own ruined face, her fingertips shredding her flesh. The guards lunged forward to stop her madness, but Arnie lashed out at them, backing up toward the only window in the room.

"Stop her!" Jax cried out, but she guessed Aranelda's plan a second too late. The crazed murderess hurled her body through the window, glass shattering and spearing toward the floor. Her screams echoed over the mountains as her body plunged down the icy chasm, crashing on the rocks hundreds of feet below.

Chapter Seventeen

Gurgling gasps from Lucien's dying lips shook Jax from her trance, tearing her eyes away from the bloody shards of the window where Aranelda had just stood. "Send for help," she commanded two of the guards who were staring in dismay at the struggling man.

"It's no use." Lucien choked back a grunt of pain. "Please, summon my children." Jax caught him as he teetered forward on his knees. "I'd like to see them. I need to apologize for all I've done."

"Why did you do it?" Darian's voice trembled at the sight of the fatal wound that had been meant for him. "Why did you stop her?"

The Duke winced as he sucked in a ragged breath. "Because of what you were willing to do." He sputtered, his cough spewing blood down the front of his tunic. "You were willing to give up your power and control to keep your lands safe. That struck a long-forgotten chord in me, I guess." He closed his eyes to better bear the pain. "And I suppose I wanted a shot at redemption for all the crimes I've committed in my sorry life."

Darian's brown irises filled with tears, nodding in silent thanks.

"What's going on? What's happened to Father?" Jax heard a chorus of questions ringing throughout the stairwell, rushing footsteps heralding the arrival of the Lysandeir triplets. She placed a comforting hand on Lysette's as she entered the room, her eyes widening at the sight. The man lying before them had been their tormentor, but at the end of the day, he was still their father.

"Come, let's leave them to say goodbye." Jax gathered her friends and left the ugliness behind.

‡

She sat nursing a glass of honeyed mead, her thoughts miles away from the conversation buzzing around her. Duke Mensina, Annette, and Darian lounged on the sofa, their softer voices lost amongst those of Duke Pettraud, Perry, George, and Roust. Jaquobie had excused himself from their little gathering to find and comfort Lysette, leaving Jax and Uma to relax in silence in the armchairs by the roaring fire.

"I know I've said this a million times tonight, but I just can't believe it." Uma's cheeks glistened with tears as she examined the firelight.

"It's all my fault." Jax felt a sharp heat spike through her chest as she admitted it out loud. "Deep down, I wanted Arnie to be dead. I wanted it all to be buried in the past, so I didn't bother having Master Vyanti confirm the body found by the lake was hers. He asked to examine the remains, you know," she paused, not having the courage to meet Uma's gaze. "But no, I wrapped her up and shipped her off to her family to be done with it. If I had just listened to him, we would have found out she was still at large." She took a long sip of the strong liquor. "My own wishful thinking was what got us here."

"You are not at fault," Uma protested, leaning forward to grasp her hand. "What Maegus and Arnie did was of their own volition. You cannot blame yourself."

"But I will." Jax gave her friend a small smile, thanking her for trying to make her feel better. She surveyed the room, her companions growing livelier, at last coming out of their shocked states. "What a disaster of a peace summit."

Uma shrugged with a slight grin. "Oh, I don't know. I think a few good things have emerged from all this misfortune."

Following Uma's gaze, Jax's eyes rested on her aunt and Darian and the tender way they held each other's hand.

Jax had been the first to concede that a dukedom was not always free of corruption, but Darian surprised her by stating Maegus's

153

treachery had proven to him that sometimes people were fooled by the person they voted for. In the end, they had come to a compromise that they planned to present jointly to the summit the following morning. Darian would assume the mantle of Cetachi, but his advisors would be made up of people elected by each tribe and region. These advisors would be charged with creating the day-to-day policies to protect and serve the Cetachi people; Darian's role as Duke was merely to oversee the carrying out of those policies. As to how he would navigate the larger political waters of the realm, Annette would be by his side to assist. While a formal engagement had not been made, both were eager to see if the chemistry between them blossomed into something more. Considering how fondly they stared at one another, Jax felt certain that the two had found their match.

"How do you think the other duchies will react, now that all of Lysandeir's bargains are off the table?" Uma's question pulled Jax back to the present.

"I think they will all fall in line, especially once they hear about the example I'm setting." Jax's lips formed a devilish grin.

Uma's brow wrinkled. "What example?"

"Uma, my dear friend, I would be honored if you would formally accept the position as my lady-in-waiting." Jax beamed with delight, clasping both of Uma's trembling hands.

"What? Jax, you're not serious, are you? I can't be a High Lady," Uma sputtered. "Have you forgotten? I'm common-born."

Jax proudly raised her chin. "From this day forward, you can be whatever you want to be, dear one. At the heart of his doctrine, Darian was right. Everyone deserves the opportunity to make something more of themselves. The color of your eyes shouldn't stand in the way of your personal achievements. For Virtues sake, we're about to have a brown-eyed Duke." She chuckled, as the change still tickled her. "It may not happen overnight, but a new era is upon us."

"What does that mean for you? For the ducal families?" Uma's concern was very real in Jax's mind also.

"We'll continue on as is, for now. But I intend to follow Cetachi's lead and allow my people to elect village leaders and representatives to send to the palace. My eyes have been opened, and I don't intend to close them now," Jax said, feeling truly content for the first time since discovering poor Marquis's body in her garden all those weeks ago.

"Hendrie will be pleased to hear that." Uma's eyes twinkled as she looked at the young man with a besotted gaze.

Jax sighed with contentment, reveling in the room filled with love.

‡

The chamber was full of anxious gazes and murmured whispers as the summit reconvened the next morning. Because of the events in the west wing tower, dinner had been served to all the guests in their suites. This morning's meeting was the first time they had been allowed out to see their colleagues, and by the incredulous looks and opened mouths around the room, word of what had happened to Duke Lysandeir and Maegus Welles was spreading.

Jax looked at Landon's tired face, his red hair not seeming to shine as brightly today. He stood at his father's seat, waiting for silence to settle over the throne room. "It is with a heavy heart that I announce the passing of my father, Lucien Alexander Loughlin, Duke of Lysandeir. The circumstances surrounding his death are a little raw, so please bear with me if I stumble." He took a deep breath, reinforcing his composure. "My father was a flawed man. But then again, so are we all. I ask, in honor of his memory, that we continue forward with our summit, as I will assume my father's throne and vote. I believe Duchess Jacqueline and the elected Governor, Darian Fangard, have a proposition they would like to push to an immediate vote."

Jax bowed her head to Landon and stood regally at her seat, Darian at her side. Together, they outlined their plan for Cetachi's future, as well as how Saphire would adopt these policies within its own borders. "We suggest reconvening this council of representatives in a year's time to report on our progress and discuss the next steps for bringing all of the realm into this new era of opportunity and prosperity."

155

With votes of support from Mensina, Saphire, Lysandeir, Pettraud, Crepsta, and Tandora, the measure passed into history.

Epilogue

Jax clung greedily to her fur cloak, the biting winds snaking through the massive stable doors. "When we reunite this time next year, remind me to advocate for someplace warmer," she said through chattering teeth. "What a glamorous sendoff." She rolled her eyes with feigned sarcasm as Darian escorted her over the straw-covered floor to her carriage.

"At least the worst of the storm has passed, and the roads are clear for your journey back, Duchess."

"When are you returning home, Duke?" Jax said, her eyebrows arched playfully.

"I'm accompanying your aunt back to Mensina, where she will collect her things before departing permanently for Cetachi." Darian ran a hand through his auburn hair, shaking his head in disbelief. "It's still a bit surreal to be called Duke. Me, the son of a baker."

She smiled with sincere warmth. "Who is now a champion for opportunity. You should be proud, Darian. You are the face of this new world."

"So are you, Jax," he protested, her nickname no longer a stranger to his lips. "Without you, none of this would have happened." He gave her arm an affectionate squeeze. "You may have thought your mind was made up, but it's always open, listening and learning. The ideal trait of a ruler."

"So, you don't think I'm completely inadequate at the job I was born into?" she teased, remembering his attacks during that first morning of the summit.

"Not completely." He chuckled before leaning in to kiss her cheek in farewell.

"See you at the wedding." Jax returned the gesture before stepping toward her awaiting carriage.

"Whose? Mine or yours?" he said with a joyful laugh before he raced back to Annette's outstretched arms.

Jax suppressed a giggle as she waved once more to her aunt and grandfather, to whom she'd bid goodbye inside the warm halls of the castle.

Duke Landon Lysandeir and his brother stood at the mountainside entrance of the stables to watch the last of the delegations depart, their red hair blowing like flames in the light wind. They had been gracious hosts while coping with the death of their father, having arranged for everyone to stay long enough to attend Landon's formal coronation a week after his father's passing. It had been a more joyous celebration than Jax had expected, especially remembering how she felt attending her own crowning. It seemed the triplets were relieved to be free of the guilt and pain their father burdened them with, both physically and emotionally.

Perry's father had left last night after the party with promises to be in Saphire at least a week before his son's wedding, and the other leaders set off for their homelands as the sun rose over the snowy mountains. Only the Cetachi, Mensina, and Saphire delegations waited until after a filling breakfast to make their leave.

Grinning at Perry, Hendrie, and George, who were already bundled up tightly on their horses, Jax hurried to the carriage door, Jaquobie's hand extending from inside to help her up the steps.

"This is cozy." Her eyes shone brightly as she gazed around the coach. Uma, sitting at her side as lady-in-waiting, masterfully hid a small giggle from everyone but Jax. Across the aisle sat Jaquobie, his hands entwined with those of his fiancée, Lysette.

The young woman looked radiant, her pink cheeks flush from the biting cold and, Jax suspected, from the adoring looks the stately High Courtier sent her way. "Thank you for making this happen,

Duchess," Lysette trilled, squeezing Jaquobie's hand in excitement. "It always seemed like such an unattainable dream for us to be together."

The tame look in Jaquobie's eyes conveyed that he, too, felt the same gratitude for all Jax had done so they could be wed during yuletide. In reality, Jax knew she couldn't take all of the credit, for Landon had been more than happy to allow his sister to travel to Saphire with the man she loved. All Jax had done was ask the newly crowned Duke to approve the engagement.

She chuckled at the sight of the beaming couple. There indeed was someone for everyone out there, it seemed. Gazing out the window, she locked eyes with Perry, the only part of his face she could see under all the layers of warm clothing. His beautiful eyes crinkled, revealing the grin hidden beneath his wool scarf. As much as she longed to see it in that moment, she planned to give him many more reasons to smile in the years to come.

Murder is a royal affair.

Discover the Court of Mystery series on eBook, audio, & paperback.

The Court of Mystery series

The Ducal Detective
A Feast Most Foul
A Voyage of Vengeance
A Summit in Shadow
Throne of Threats
Paradise Plagued
Burdened Bloodline
Sovereign Sieged
Crown of Chaos
Harrowed Heir
Ravaged Reign
Innocence Imprisoned
Ardent Ascension
Eternal Empire

More Cozy Mysteries by Sarah

Trending Topic Mysteries
Glenmyre Whim Mysteries
Book Blogger Mysteries

www.saraheburr.com

Acknowledgments

Many thanks to Bettye Underwood for her copyedit and review, making sure my words thoughtfully illustrated the jumble of feelings I have about all my characters.

Thank you to Elizabeth Orlando and her second-grade class for making me feel like a real author for the first time in my life.

A special thank you to Mihail Uvarov, the designer of the original series covers. Your depictions of Jax will always hold a special place in my heart.

Dedication

To the Duchess's growing fanbase

About the Author

Sarah E. Burr has been dreaming of being Nancy Drew since her small-town days in Appleton, Maine—but when corporate America didn't deliver any mysteries, she started writing her own! Now an award-winning author, Sarah pens the Book Blogger Mysteries, Court of Mystery series, and the fan-favorite Trending Topic Mysteries and Glenmyre Whim Mysteries. Her cozy crafting caper, *You Can't Candle the Truth,* was a 2022 finalist for both the NGIBA and Silver Falchion awards, while *#TagMe for Murder* was a 2024 NGIBA finalist for Best Click Lit Fiction.

A proud Sisters in Crime member, Sarah also runs BookstaBundles, a content creation service for authors. She co-hosts *It's Bookish Time TV*, a cozy web channel full of fun author interviews, and blogs for *Writers Who Kill*.

When not plotting her next whodunit, Sarah sings show tunes, plays video games with her husband, and takes long walks with her adorable pup, Eevee. Want free short stories and exclusive updates? Join her newsletter here: https://bit.ly/saraheburrbookssignup.